His eyes blazed with a strange, fierce light. "Say my name!" He gave her a brusque shake. "Damn you, Abigail, say it."

His gaze seemed to burn into hers, compelling her.

"Nathaniel," she whispered, and she knew the moment his name escaped her lips she was lost. His mouth crashed down on hers, hot and avid.

Abigail moaned low in her throat, trying to resist the dizzying fury of Nate's kiss. But she felt her hands slowly slipping further and further up the wall of his chest until her arms wound round his neck, until nothing separated them but the thin barrier of their clothing.

Also by Susan Carroll
Published by Fawcett Books:

THE LADY WHO HATED SHAKESPEARE
THE SUGAR ROSE
BRIGHTON ROAD
THE BISHOP'S DAUGHTER
THE WOOING OF MISS MASTERS
MISTRESS MISCHIEF
CHRISTMAS BELLES

MISS PRENTISS
AND
THE YANKEE

Susan Carroll

FAWCETT CREST • NEW YORK

A Fawcett Crest Book
Published by Ballantie Books
Copyright © 1993 by Susan Coppula

Library of Congress Catalog Card Number: 93-90532

ISBN 0-449-22074-5

Manufactured in the United States of America

First Edition: December 1993

Chapter 1

"Hellfire and damnation!"

Nate Harding's blue eyes fired with outrage as he scanned the newspaper unfolded on the mahogany desk of his study. The *Gazette* was over two months old, crumpled and weather-stained, showing signs of its lengthy passage from the distant shores of Philadelphia to this secluded manor house in the rolling hills of Buckinghamshire, England.

But the newsprint retained its clarity, the bold black words of the editorial seeming to leap off the page. After reading it, Nate shoved to his feet with such force, he sent a stack of correspondence flying off the desk, all the missives addressed to the Honorable Nathaniel Lawrence Harding. The title set as uncomfortably with the very American Mr. Harding as the tight-fitting tailcoat he had discarded earlier. The much-abused garment lay heaped upon the floor with its companion waistcoat and the disheveled remains of a starched cravat.

Snatching up the newspaper, he trampled over both the clothing and the letters as he paced around the desk. Reading the article again, Nate dragged his hand through the shagged lengths of his ash blond hair.

"Hellfire and damnation," he repeated. Rolling the paper up, he slapped it against the palm of his hand. "Piracy! That's what it is. Nothing more than barefaced piracy."

His mouth hardened, which only served to accent the stubborn jut of his chin. He had a strong face, his complexion too deeply tanned, his jawline too square, his eyebrows too heavy to be accounted classically handsome. His nose was slightly crooked owing to having been broken a time or two, a not unexpected consequence for a man too ready with his fists and his tongue.

The infamous Harding temper simmered close to the surface as Nate strode up and down the room, growling imprecations about "British tyrants! Blackguards! Cursed injustice!" But the fire irons and the portrait of some dour English ancestor hung above the mantel offered a cold and unsympathetic audience. Tucking the paper under his arm, Nate charged out of the study in quest of someone to share his indignation.

He had not taken more than a few steps down the hall when servants seemed to melt out of the woodwork, bowing and curtsying, all eager to be of service to Ashdown Manor's new master. Nate could not put names to over half of them yet nor did he have the least idea what they did besides wait in ambush for him. He'd have preferred facing a party of hostile Creek Indians. Far better that than being done to death by an excess of civility.

As Nate approached the crimson drawing room, one scrawny fellow—Andrew, Nate believed he was called—sprang forward to get there ahead of Nate.

As near as Nate could tell, the chap lived for nothing but to strut about in his powdered wig and fancy livery, opening doors.

Upon his arrival at Ashdown Manor a fortnight ago, Nate had tartly informed Andrew that he had managed to open his own doors for thirty-one years now, thank you very much. But the little fellow had looked so crushed that Nate had recanted, learning to tolerate the small service.

Andrew swept open the imposing double doors leading into the drawing room with a bow and a grand flourish. Nate grimaced but managed to nod his thanks as he crossed over the threshold.

His two young half sisters were just where Nate had left them after breakfast. Clarice's dark head was bent over her workbasket as she mended a torn lace tucker. Louisa sat at the pianoforte, fumbling over the keys.

Nate marveled that they could look so at home here in this room that was as alien to him as the rest of the house. A lush blend of blue, red, and gold, the drawing room looked as though it belonged in the palace of a king.

And Americans didn't hold with palaces or kings.

But he had to remember his sisters were much younger and more impressionable than he, Louisa only eighteen and Clarice just turned sixteen that past summer. Impatiently tapping his newspaper, Nate crossed over to Clarice ensconced on the settee. He was immediately taken aback by the blaze of logs upon the floor.

"Damn!" he said, tugging at the collar of his linen shirt. "It's like an inferno in here."

"We were cold," Louisa called out, tossing her

auburn-tinted curls over her shoulder as she leaned forward to peer at her sheets of music.

"Small wonder," Nate groused. "If you will persist in running around in those scanty muslin dresses. It's almost October for Chrissakes."

"My!" Louisa said. "Aren't we as cross as a bee-stung bear!"

Clarice glanced up from her sewing to regard Nate with her soft dove gray eyes. "Are you not having a good morning, Nate?"

"No, I decidedly am not!" He thrust the newspaper forward for her inspection. "Only look what Mr. Thomas sent me from back home, an issue of the *Gazette*. Just read the editorial." Giving her no chance to do so, he continued, "The cursed British navy has been at it again, intercepting American vessels at sea."

"What a shame." Clarice sighed. "It's a deal too bad of them, Nate."

"Too bad? It's abominable! It says right here that British naval officers boarded the *Speedwell* by force on the flimsy pretext of searching for deserters. . . ." Nate trailed off, realizing from Clarice's puzzled look she was not comprehending the significance of all this. She was a sweet girl, but not half so quick as Louisa.

Turning aside, he stalked over to the pianoforte and continued, "Just listen to this, Lou. The British seized six American sailors off the *Speedwell*, impressed them into His Royal High and Mightiness's navy. It's an outrage."

"It certainly is," Louisa sniffed. She left off tinkering with the keys to frown up at Nate. "Speaking of outrages, what have you done with your fine new coat and waistcoat, Nate Harding?"

"Waistcoats be hanged at a time like this! American trade is being threatened, American citizens are being kidnapped—"

"You can't run around in your shirtsleeves here, Nate," Louisa persisted. "Miss Prentiss would never approve. This isn't Pennsylvania."

"I wish to God it was," Nate said bitterly. A wave of homesickness washed over him, stronger than any he had experienced during the three months since he'd first set foot on accursed British soil. Back home, he could well imagine the heat and energy with which this outrage regarding the *Speedwell* was being debated, in the cobblestone streets of Philadelphia, the inns, the taverns, the grog shops. . . .

Or rather how this event would have been discussed two months ago, Nate thought glumly regarding the faded date. Who knew what latest excitement was spreading through the streets of that bustling city today? His city, or so it once had been.

He conjured up a vision of the bustling wharves, the masts of the ships in Philadelphia harbor piercing the city skyline, the tree-lined avenues, the snug brick houses, the crowded market places, the spire of Independence Hall, the very cradle of American liberties. Nate sighed, feeling very much cut adrift from home, from country, from any kindred spirit who seemed capable of entering into his feelings.

He knew a brief flickering of hope when Louisa paused in her playing to frown. "I suppose if the British keep up this nonsense of bothering our ships, it could lead to war."

"Yes, indeed it could," Nate said. "The president

5

and Congress will not be able to tolerate this sort of thing much longer. The English persist in treating us as though we were still their blasted colonists. We fought one war to throw off the yoke of tyranny, and we won't hesitate to—"

"Well, I just hope the president doesn't do anything odious before we have a chance to enjoy our first London Season."

Nate stared at Louisa for a moment in disbelief before snapping, "Oh, I'll send President Madison a letter straightaway, warning him that no matter how many American seamen are abducted, he must do nothing that would upset the God-cursed Season over here."

"Don't swear so much, Nate," Louisa said loftily as she resumed her playing. "I don't think Miss Prentiss will like it."

"Whoever the devil she might be!"

"I would not like missing the Season either, Nate," Clarice ventured timidly. "But if you think a war might be more important . . ."

Nate scarce heard her as he stomped over to the fire. In a gesture of pure frustration, he consigned the newspaper to the flames.

Louisa faltered over the next note and complained, "I think we need a new pianoforte."

"And from the amount of bills on my desk this morning," Nate said, "I think we have been spending enough money over here, lining these fat British merchants' pockets."

"But Miss Prentiss says a lady can never learn to play well unless she has a truly capital instrument."

"There's nothing wrong with the instrument, only your playing." Irritably, Nate stalked up be-

6

hind Louisa. Locating the note she was seeking, he plunked it himself with a resounding clang. "And who the deuce *is* this Miss Prentiss you keep talking about?"

"Our new governess."

"What!"

Instead of answering, Louisa swept away from the pianoforte, suddenly consumed by a great need to rearrange the Dresden figurines on the sofa table.

"I can play that piece better than Louisa, Nate," Clarice said. "I have been practicing."

Setting aside her sewing, she eagerly assumed Louisa's vacated place at the pianoforte, but Nate had already stalked after his eldest sister.

"What governess, Louisa?" he demanded.

"The one we engaged while we were in town last month."

"And why the blazes wasn't I consulted about this?"

Louisa shrugged. "I daresay you were too busy with some of your horrid business meetings or in consultation with the solicitors. And you did give me and Clarice leave to shop for whatever we needed."

"So you plucked some female off the shelf like you were purchasing a new hat! What the deuce do you want with a governess? You and Clarice graduated from one of the finest ladies' seminaries in Philadelphia."

"But, Nate, Miss Prentiss is a most superior kind of governess," Clarice put in. "However, if you don't approve—"

"Don't be a dolt, Clarrie," Louisa said. "Why shouldn't Nate approve? We need Miss Prentiss to teach us how to get on in society. When she interviewed us in London, she could see that we had much to learn before we are presented next spring."

"When *she* interviewed you!"

"Miss Prentiss is much sought after. She has an excellent reputation for preparing young ladies who are about to make their debut in London. And she charges a mere sixty pounds per annum."

"Sixty pounds!" Nate roared. He did a rapid mental calculation, translating this into American dollars. "Hellfire and damnation! Do you know how many laborers Uncle Frank could have engaged in the shipyards back home for such a sum?"

"It's not the same thing at all. Miss Prentiss has been both tutor and companion to dukes' and earls' daughters. It is a great honor that she would deign to bother with us at all."

"She can do her deigning elsewhere. We have enough useless people wandering about this house. I'm not wasting good money to bring in another one."

Louisa scowled at him. "Don't keep going on about money, Nate. This is not Pennsylvania. It's considered vulgar over here to fret over costs. It makes you sound like a Yankee trader."

"I *am* a Yankee trader. Too shrewd to be fleeced by some high-toned, pinched-nose governess."

"Oh, no!" Clarice said. "Miss Prentiss has a very nice nose, Nate. She's so elegant, so refined, so—so cultivated."

"From the sound of her, I can't abide her already!"

"That's a great pity," Louisa said, squaring off

8

with Nate. "Because we've already sent the best carriage in the stables to fetch her from London."

"The best carriage can turn right around and fetch her back there again."

Louisa pressed forward until she and Nate were standing toe-to-toe, glaring. She barely came up to his shoulder, but what she lacked in inches she made up for in truculence.

"I might have known you would be disagreeable," she said. "It wouldn't hurt you to take a few lessons from Miss Prentiss yourself on how to be a gentleman."

"There's nothing any stiff-lipped British female can teach me, or my sisters for that matter, and when this infernal Miss Prentiss arrives, I'll be happy to tell her so."

Louisa's eyes glittered with tears, but Nate was not fooled into any expression of sympathy. When Louisa was angry enough to be close to weeping, she was just as close to slugging him one. Although Clarice hastened over, attempting to soothe both of them, her efforts were ignored as Louisa shrilled, "And just how do you expect Clarice and me to get on in society if you send Miss Prentiss packing?"

"The same as you did back in Philadelphia. And if these plaguey English aristocrats cannot accept us as we are, then the devil with all of them."

"It's different here," Louisa said, stomping her foot. "*Ohhh*, I could just box your ears, Nate, when you get this stubborn. This isn't Pennsylvania."

"It's me who will box your ears if you say that one more time—"

"Is anything amiss, my dears?"

The low pleasant voice coming from the doorway was finally loud enough to make itself heard above

Louisa and Nate's heated argument. Lady Helen Harding's gentle question had the effect of producing immediate silence.

Nate turned toward the slender woman who had slipped into the room. His stepmother smiled even though her brow was furrowed with concern. She looked tired and pale again this morning, though perhaps it was only by contrast to her black gown. Helen was still a lovely woman for all that her face was too thin, her dark hair flecked with gray. He was going to have to find some way to coax her out of her mourning, Nate thought. He knew his father would have wished him to do so.

Crossing the room, he took Helen by the hand and bade her good morning, pressing a kiss to her cheek with a gentleness he rarely showed anyone.

"Did we disturb you with our fracas, ma'am?" he asked. " 'Tis nothing for you to worry about, I promise. Only me and Louisa having another of our set-tos."

"Nate is threatening to turn off our Miss Prentiss, Mama," Louisa said indignantly, "before she even gets here. He said—"

"Can you credit it, Nell?" Nate interrupted. "These silly chits hired a governess while we were in London. Of all the ridiculous waste of good money!"

A hint of color stained Lady Helen's cheeks. "I am afraid that it is not precisely true, Nathaniel. It was I who engaged Miss Prentiss."

"You?" Nate stared at her, thunderstruck.

Helen cleared her throat. "Er—girls, perhaps you might want to take a walk in the garden. I need to speak to your brother alone."

"But Mama," Louisa protested, "there is no need

for all this botheration. Nate is only being cross and disagreeable because Mr. Thomas sent him another Philadelphia newspaper, and the British navy is stopping American ships again. And you know what Nate is like when he gets on his patriotic high horse—"

"Louisa! That will do, child," Lady Helen said.

But Helen was often too soft-spoken to make much impression on the stubborn Louisa. It was left to Nate to hustle both girls from the room, firmly closing the door in the face of Louisa's pout.

Helen heaved a wearied sigh, but Nate would hear none of her explanations until he had settled her on the wing-back chair next to the hearth. Slipping a footstool beneath her feet, he barraged her with questions.

"How are you feeling today? Did you sleep well? Did you take any breakfast? Shall I get you something? There's an army of servants out there. Surely one of them can manage a cup of tea. Or I could brew you up some of my Grandmama Buckmeister's herbal remedy. It's very restorative—"

"No, no, just send for a mustard plaster and some liniment to rub into my creaking joints." Lady Helen chuckled. She had a light musical laugh. Gazing fondly at Nate, she said, "You foolish boy! You fuss over me worse than the nurse I had when I was a little girl."

"You need a deal of fussing over," Nate said. But his sternness was belied by his grin. "You are a most fractious patient."

Veiling his concern, Nate subsided, drawing up a straight-backed chair for himself, well away from the fire. This was the first day since their arrival at

Ashdown Manor that Nell had arisen from her bed this early.

The voyage across the Atlantic had been hard on her, and all the traveling about they had done since then had not helped matters. Their brief sojourn in London had been particularly bad. Too much heat, dampness, and that infernal fog. After their final leg of their journey here to Ashdown Manor, she had been done in and was only slowly recovering her strength.

But Nell always had been of a delicate constitution unlike the hearty daughter of a wealthy Pennsylvania farmer who had been Nate's mother. He'd heard it said that Bess Buckmeister had never known a sick day in her life until the virulent attack of typhus that had caused her death.

Nate's memories of his mother were no longer so clear. He recalled a jolly golden-haired woman, strong and strapping. He remembered the feel of her gentle, work-roughened hands stroking his hair back from his forehead. And he remembered the devastation he had felt when she died.

A devastation so great it had left him belligerent and intolerant of the English lady his father had proposed to, to take his mother's place. He had turned his back on Lady Helen when the late Lord John Harding had first brought her out to the farm. Nate had refused to even look at her.

But Helen had been mighty patient with the stubborn, grief-stricken eleven-year-old boy.

"I know I can never replace your mama, Nathaniel," she had said. "You may call me Helen, and I only hope you will let me be your friend . . . in time."

In time.

Nate's lips curved softly at the memory. He had never been sure how or when it had happened over the succeeding years. But in time Helen had become *Nell*.

As he studied her now, it amused him to see his regal-looking step-mama appearing rather guilty, like a little girl caught out in some mischief.

"About Miss Prentiss, Nathaniel," she began. "I meant to tell you about her sooner, but we have all been so distracted since our departure from London, it slipped my mind. Unpardonable, I know, to be engaging a governess without consulting you, but I do intend to pay her salary myself and—"

"Nell, Nell," Nate scolded. "You know I'd hire you a dozen governesses if you wanted them. But what in heaven's name do you want one for?"

"Miss Prentiss is a superior young woman."

"So I have been told," Nate said dryly.

"She comes from a very good family. Her sister is Lady Longsford and her brother, I believe, is a well-respected gentleman who married a baronet's daughter."

"If this Miss Prentiss has such high and mighty relatives, why isn't she my lady something or other herself by now?"

"I don't know, my dear. I did not feel it right to pry further into her background."

"Pry! Nell, you were interviewing her for a post in your household. You had a right to ask what questions you pleased."

Helen looked somewhat abashed, and Nate sought to curb his exasperated tone. But it was clear to him that this governess female had run roughshod over his mild-mannered step-mama already. He had a strong presentiment that someone would be obliged to haul back on Miss Prentiss's reins, and that someone would most likely have to be him.

Lady Helen continued, "The important thing about Miss Prentiss, Nathaniel, is her reputation. And that speaks clearly for itself. She is noted for turning her charges into elegant young ladies, well able to survive the ordeal of being presented to society. Oh, Nathaniel, you can have no idea what it is like for a girl facing her first Season in London."

"But you could teach Louisa and Clarice all that rubbish yourself, couldn't you? You had a Season before you came over to America."

Helen smiled ruefully. "So I did, but I was not a great success. Such a timid little mouse, I attracted little notice from anyone, certainly not the gentlemen. Of course, that turned out for the best. Otherwise, I never would have accompanied my papa when he came to take up his diplomatic post in America, and I never would have met your father."

"Well, there then. You see!" Nate spread his hands in a triumphant gesture.

"But a Season in London can be a wonderful experience. I would like my girls to enjoy all the excitement of it far better than I did."

Nate squirmed beneath the wistful expression in Nell's gray eyes. "But you really think we need some snobbish governess coming here, to lord her fancy manners over us? And at such a sum. Sixty pounds!"

"Miss Prentiss knows her own worth, and I've never seen you fault anyone for that, Nathaniel." Lady Helen said. "I've also never seen you deny your sisters anything they wanted. You spoil them far worse than I do. I've a notion you don't care about Miss Prentiss one way or the other."

After a pause, she added, "What is it that is really troubling you, dear heart?"

Nate lowered his eyes, seeking to avoid Helen's clear-eyed gaze. His gentle step-mama had always possessed the ability to see far too much.

"Nothing. Nothing at all, ma'am," he said, striving for an easy laugh.

Lady Helen wasn't fooled. "Louisa mentioned something about a newspaper. Was there bad news from Philadelphia?"

"Only the usual reports about the accursed British stopping ships again—" Nate broke off, flushing. "I'm sorry, Nell. I keep forgetting that some of these people are your relatives."

"And yours."

Nate chose to ignore that comment.

"You truly do not like it here, do you?" Helen persisted.

Nate rose from his chair, paced off a few steps, affecting a careless shrug. "What's not to like? I suddenly find myself lord of an English country estate with everyone bowing and scraping to me like I was the Grand Potentate of the Ottoman Empire. It's everything my father ever dreamed of."

"I fear that is exactly what is amiss," Helen said. "It was your father's dream, not yours."

Nate nodded tersely. That was the bitter irony of it all, he thought. That word of his family's forgiveness and this English inheritance should only have reached the Lord John Alexander Douglass Harding as he lay dying. So many years spent in exile and then on one's deathbed, to see one's dream finally fulfilled, to have no son to pass it on to except one very stubborn, ungrateful Yankee.

Helen continued, "I know your father would never have wanted you to be this restless and unhappy. I fear his mind was not clear during his last hours or he would not have asked such a sacrifice from you, extracted such a promise."

"He only asked me to pledge that I would come over and check upon the estate, sample the delights of his precious England for one year before deciding how to dispose of the property."

"A year can be a long time for a young man," Helen said sympathetically.

Indeed, it could be. A year in which Nate had had many plans: for joining his uncle Franklin Buckmeister as a partner in the shipping business; for setting into motion the architectural plans he had drawn up for turning the old family farmhouse on the outskirts of Philadelphia into something that would rival Jefferson's Monticello; for sounding out the local politicians on the chances of one Mr. Nathaniel Harding making a bid for a seat in Congress. As a promising young lawyer himself, and being the grandson of that great Revolutionary war hero, Colonel Hans Sebastian Buckmeister, Nate had been told his chances of election were very good.

Nate sighed, putting all such notions out of his head for now. They would keep.

"A year of my life was not so much for my father to ask," he said, assuring himself as much as Helen. "I owed him that much."

And more. Nate felt the familiar stirrings of guilt and remorse, still as sharp as they had been eighteen months ago when he attended the deathbed of his father; that quiet soul Nathaniel had to admit he had never really known or understood; that— that *Englishman* he had at times felt vaguely ashamed of.

With such troubled thoughts chasing through his head, Nate glanced up to find Nell regarding him, her eyes clouded. He gave himself a brisk mental shake, striving for a more cheerful mien. He would not have Lady Helen worrying about him or spoil her pleasure in her own homecoming for anything.

Crossing to her side, he caught up her hand and pressed it. "You must not fret about me, Nell. I shall survive. After all, there are only nine more months to go. And I will say this for your England, when it isn't raining, there are some damned fine hills for riding—"

He brought himself up short, his lips twitching with mischief. "No, I forget I must learn to mind my oaths. Miss Prentiss might not like it."

"Nate, if you truly do not care for the idea of Miss Prentiss coming here—"

"Nay, madam, bring on your English governess. Who knows? She might contrive to teach Louisa something more of geography. The only point the girl seems clear on is"—Nate mimicked in a high falsetto—"*'This is not Pennsylvania.'*"

Lady Helen chuckled at that. It was good to hear her ready to laugh again, to see some color stealing into her cheeks. If she was happy to be here at Ashdown Manor, if the girls were likewise content, Nate supposed he too could muddle through the rest of the year.

Helping Helen to her feet, Nate inquired after Helen's plans for the day.

"I received an invitation," she said, her gray eyes sparkling with an almost girlish pleasure. "From Lady Sophia Blake. She and I went to school together, oh, so many years ago. She is settled not far from here. And she begs that I will bring my girls and come for a visit."

"That sounds an excellent notion. I'll allow you to go on one condition. You fetch one of your prettier gowns and bonnets from your wardrobe."

"Nathaniel! As if you have ever paid any heed to feminine finery."

"No, but I know what I don't like. I detest black, and I'm not fond of a deal of lace on a lady's bodice either, hiding all her charms."

"Wicked rogue!" Helen gave his arm a playful smack, but she sighed almost immediately. "I am not at all sure I should accept Sophia's invitation, at least not today."

"Why not? You could not have a fairer day for traveling, cool and crisp, the sun still shining."

"But I am not certain when Miss Prentiss will arrive. It would be dreadful if none of us were here to greet her."

"None of us! I would be here. The lord of the manor. I will contrive to give her a warm welcome."

"What? With a salvo from your grandpapa's old musket?"

"No! You know I can be perfectly charming with the ladies when I choose," Nate said, summoning up his most roguish smile.

"Ye-e-ss," Helen agreed. But as Nate escorted her from the room, she struggled to hide a fluttering of trepidation.

It was quite true. When he chose to do so, Nate could be quite a charmer, the perfect gentleman.

But it was likewise true, when Nate chose otherwise, the man could be a perfect devil.

Chapter 2

The coach teetered at an odd angle, the rim of the back wheel in splinters. Only the sedate pace of the horses at the time the wheel had cracked had saved the carriage from being overturned completely. But the coachman looked as gloom-ridden as though it were a total disaster. The footman who had been thrown from his perch on the rear, winced and rubbed his arm. The team of horses pawed nervously in their traces.

The only one who appeared unruffled by the carriage mishap was its sole passenger. Helped from the interior of the coach, Miss Abigail Prentiss was still the picture of calm and cool elegance. She smoothed out the folds of her navy blue pelisse with hands encased in immaculate kid gloves, then straightened the broad brim of her bonnet.

She had fine-boned features, high cheekbones, and a nose that it pleased her to describe as "aristocratic." Her face might reasonably have been expected to be pale after such a fright, but her complexion retained its smooth peaches and cream tint.

Not a strand of her raven-colored hair was even out of place. It was swept back into a severe style calculated to downplay any pretensions of being called handsome; Miss Prentiss had learned long ago that beauty was not a quality much valued in a governess.

She walked to the rear of the coach and surveyed the damage through intelligent green eyes.

The coachman, Mr. Horrick, clicked his tongue and shook his head. " 'Tis the most ill-fated thing in the world, miss, and with us but yards from the end of our journey."

It was quite true. They were actually within the park gates of Ashdown Manor. The redbrick house with its gleaming white window casements could be seen in the distance across a regal sweep of green lawn.

"I knew as how that wheel should've been looked to before we ever left London," the footman muttered.

The coachman glared at him, but before any altercation could develop between the two men, Abigail stepped smoothly into the breach.

"Never mind, Mr. Horrick," she soothed. "We may count ourselves fortunate that this mishap has occurred so close to the house. You'd best get the horses unhitched and up to the stables.

"Daniel," she said turning to the footman. "You should go to the house and alert some of the other men to come down and help. And have your arm tended to at once. It is not broken, but I daresay you have a nasty sprain."

"Yes, miss."

Both men were quick to concur with her instructions and indeed looked rather relieved. Abigail supposed they were grateful to discover that their female passenger was not going to succumb to hysterics.

But hysterics were quite foreign to Abigail Prentiss's nature. She was accustomed to taking charge, dealing with any catastrophe, setting things to rights. She could likely have even told them how to fix the wheel if she took the time to study it properly.

But her most immediate problem was to get both herself and her trunks the rest of the way to Ashdown Manor. Shading her eyes, she glanced toward the distant house, basking serenely in the afternoon sun. Her lips quirked in a wry smile as she imagined that there were several disgruntled women in London who would say her present difficulty served her quite right.

Both Lady Summerville and the Countess of Ainswick had been vexed with Abigail when she had turned down offers from their august houses to accept the position with the Hardings instead.

Lady Summerville had been particularly shrill in her disappointment and disapproval.

"Governess to *Americans*," her ladyship had cried, in the same tone some ancient Roman dame might have described hoards of invading Huns. "They will be positive savages, Miss Prentiss. Boisterous, uncivilized, vulgar. What can you be thinking of?"

But Abigail had found that a more apt description of her ladyship's own brood. And as for the Hardings, after several interviews, Abigail had determined Lady Harding and her daughters to be not in the least savage, but most charming.

Of course, there was a son Abigail had not met.

But as governess, she could hardly be expected to have anything to do with the young gentleman of the house.

It promised to be a pleasant employment, tucked away here in the quiet and peace of the countryside. And though some might regard the carriage accident as an ill omen, Abigail was not in the least daunted or apprehensive that she might have erred by coming here.

It was a well-known fact that Abigail Prentiss did not make errors. Or at least she had very rarely in the course of her eight and twenty years. There had been that one painful episode in the Duke of Rivington's household, her very first employment. But she had been so young then, so foolish and inexperienced.

Abigail's mouth trembled a little at the memory of those days, bittersweet and laced with thoughts of things that might have been. But she shook off the mood, taking herself sharply to task. This was hardly the time and place to be going all soft and sentimental.

The coachman was still struggling to get the team out of harness, and there was no sign of Daniel. Abigail wondered if he had succeeded in alerting the house as yet. She was considering marching forward to do so herself when she saw the figure of a man striding across the lawn.

He was tall with excessively broad shoulders, and he put Abigail strangely in mind of English yeomen of yore, those bold strapping fellows who had once tramped the woods in the company of the legendary Robin of the Hood. She half expected to see him toting a longbow, a brace of arrows strapped to his back.

Abigail chided herself for her fancifulness, but as the man came closer, the notion would not be dispelled. Sunlight struck through the trees, glinting on his ash blond hair. The gold-threaded strands hung well past his collar only adding to his appearance of being rough and untamed.

His skin was bronzed a deep tan, his white shirtsleeves pushed up to reveal a pair of brawny forearms. And his breeches were the most curious garment Abigail had ever seen, a soft doeskin with leather fringes down the side. They outlined with vivid clarity the well-honed contours of his thighs and—

And Abigail brought herself up short. Ogling muscular stable hands was something she rebuked her young pupils for doing, not a pastime in which she herself indulged. And a stable hand of some sort is what this man had to be.

As he strode up to the coach, he cast Abigail a cursory glance, but most of his attention was reserved for the tilted carriage. The coachman was just leading the team of horses away along the drive that meandered back to the house.

Placing his hands on the flat planes of his hips, the rugged-looking groom frowned. "What happened here? Was anybody hurt?"

"No, thankfully not," Abigail spoke up. "The footman did sprain his arm a little, but I have already sent him to the house. And as you can see, the coachman is taking care of the horses. If you wish to make yourself useful, you could fetch my small trunk down. I can make do without the rest for the present."

The man shifted toward her then, his eyes cool and assessing. Abigail noted they were blue, very blue, and raked her with a boldness she was not accustomed to from stable yard help.

"I am Miss Abigail Prentiss, the new governess," she said. "Lady Harding will be expecting me."

This announcement should have produced a more respectful attitude in the man, but it didn't. He folded his arms across his chest, looked her up and down one more time, then pursed his lips in a low, appreciative whistle.

He muttered something that sounded like, "The new governess. I'll be damned. Well, the sight of that figure alone might be worth the sixty pounds."

"I beg your pardon," Abigail said icily.

He gave her a disarming grin. "If I had ever had a schoolmistress as pretty as you, I doubt I could have paid a scrap of attention to my lessons."

Abigail froze him with her best governess-like stare. "If I had ever been your teacher, sir, rest assured I would have made certain that you did so."

He chuckled, a deep rich sound. Thoroughly affronted, Abigail was tempted to give him a stinging setdown. But she could tell from his strange accent, he must be a servant the Hardings had brought over with them from America. As such, Abigail supposed that allowances had to be made.

"If you would be so good as to fetch my trunk," she said, "I would like to present myself to Lady Harding."

"I am afraid that's not possible. She and the girls went off to visit some Lady Thingamabob. They likely won't be back until late this evening."

"Then is young Mr. Harding available?" Abigail asked with strained patience.

"Oh, yes, ma'am. Very," he said with a wolfish grin. Even the corners of his eyes seemed to crinkle with amusement. Abigail's forbearance with the man was about to snap when he confounded her by sweeping one arm across his chest in a gallant bow.

"Young Mr. Harding at your service, ma'am." The gravity of his expression was belied by the devils dancing in his eyes.

It took Abigail a moment to comprehend what he was saying. Then she cried out in disbelief, "You? The Honorable Nathaniel Harding. Impossible!"

"Where I come from, ma'am, a man can be honorable with no need of a fancy title affixed to his name to prove it. But, yes, I am indeed Nate Harding."

He took her hand in a strong grasp, clearly enjoying her discomfiture. His skin pulsed warm with the life's blood of a very hearty, lusty male. She could feel the power of his grip, the heat of his flesh even through her glove.

Drawing her hand back from the disturbing contact, she said, "You might have told me who you were at once, Mr. Harding."

"I don't recollect as you ever troubled to ask, Mistress Abigail." He smiled down at her, but there was no malice in his eyes. Rather they were warm, inviting her to share in his little jest, but Abigail did not enjoy being made to feel foolish.

"I am sorry," she said stiffly. "Perhaps I should have been able to guess your identity, but I thought—that is I rather expected that you would be younger."

"Hellfire, ma'am! I am scarcely in my dotage."

"What I mean is that I supposed you would be nearer in age to your sisters. If I had been at all prepared, I would not have mistaken you for one of the stable hands."

"Don't fret about it. It happens to me all the time."

"I daresay."

He continued to grin at her, but when Abigail met his overtures with a chilling silence, his own smile faded.

"I guess you are still waiting on me to fetch that trunk you mentioned." He pivoted on his heel and headed for the back of the carriage.

"Oh, no!" Abigail trailed after him, horrified. "Of course, I would never have asked you to do so, Mr. Harding if I had known— But stay a moment, sir. I am certain Daniel will send one of the footmen down from the house and—"

"Oh, I expect they are all too busy with their door-opening and silver-polishing. I doubt any of those English fellows would be much use for something like this."

Abigail did not miss the scornful emphasis Mr. Harding placed on the word *English*, but she was far too distracted by the sight of the master of Ashdown Manor hoisting down her trunk and balancing it upon his broad shoulder.

"Pray, Mr. Harding, don't. This is not necessary—"

But he was already striding away, heading back through the trees toward the lawn. He paused only long enough to glance back.

"Coming?" he demanded before setting off again. Abigail was left with no choice but to follow.

She hastened after him, marveling that he could set such a pace while wielding her heavy trunk. Not only that, Abigail noted with pursed lips, he could balance the chest with apparently little effort and still manage to swagger at the same time.

As they neared the house, she saw that word of

the carriage accident must have spread, for several of the servants had come out of the manor.

One of the footmen raced forward to relieve Mr. Harding of the trunk, but he waved the servant impatiently aside. He shifted the trunk a little, flexing his back muscles until the linen of his shirt was strained taut. Abigail began to wonder just whom Mr. Harding was showing off for, herself or some of the pert, giggling housemaids.

As some of the footmen also snickered, Abigail's cheeks heated. She felt relieved when they finally reached the manor's doorstep. A scrawny bewigged servant raced ahead to fling open the large oak portal.

"Thank you, Andrew," Mr. Harding said, pulling a rather odd face.

Abigail trailed after him into the cool interior of the manor's entry hall. Heavy oak stairs rose up in landings at right angles leading to the upper floor. Mr. Harding plunked her trunk down with such carelessness, it skidded a little ways upon the highly polished scagliola floor. Abigail winced, wondering if she would find her hand mirror and bottles of toilet water still intact.

Mr. Harding stepped around the abandoned chest, calling out orders to some of the servants to go see about getting that carriage moved off the drive.

"And tell Mrs. Bridges I'll be wanting to see her. We need to get one of the bedchambers readied for Mistress Abigail and—" He spun around to face Abigail. "You'll be wanting some refreshment after your journey. Tea most likely?"

"A cup of tea would be lovely," Abigail said, then wondered if Mr. Harding proposed to make it himself. After that performance with her trunk, she would not put anything past him. Perhaps he was even planning to turn down her sheets. The thought of those large, weather-toughened hands smoothing back her bed linens brought a strange fluttering to the pit of Abigail's stomach.

"Mr. Harding," she said, "in the face of your mother's absence, perhaps the best thing to do would be simply to turn me over to your housekeeper. I would hardly expect you to look after me."

"No? Well, maybe I would just like the pleasure of your company for a few moments, Mistress Abigail." He shoved open a door that she could see led to a small parlor.

"I—I don't think—" she began.

"Unless you are afraid to be alone in the same room with me? I suppose someone's been filling your head with stories about us savage, uncivilized Americans."

"No, of course not," Abigail said, feeling a telltale blush creep up her cheeks. "I would not credit such tales even if they did."

"Good. Then you won't mind talking with me for a few minutes, answering a few questions. I know you must be tired, and I promise not to keep you long."

It was a civil request, and Abigail did not see how she could refuse it. Even if Mr. Harding had been a perfect savage, he could hardly pounce upon her in a houseful of servants. Could he?

Quelling an inexplicable stirring of unease, Abigail allowed him to usher her into the parlor. It was a light, airy chamber, its hangings a bright yellow. Mr. Harding strode with some impatience over to the tall windows and began flinging open the drapes.

"I don't know why the maids around here insist upon shutting up all the rooms this way," he complained.

"It's the afternoon light, Mr. Harding," Abigail said. "It can fade the furnishings."

"I don't see that a few sticks of old furniture matter in comparison to being cut off from the sun."

A few sticks of old furniture? Abigail cringed as she watched bright sunlight pour across the green brocade of an elegant-carved settee that had to have dated from the Queen Anne period. But she managed to hold her tongue.

"Have a seat, Mistress Abigail," he said.

She supposed he meant it as an invitation, but it came out more like a command, especially since he all but thrust an elegantly carved Hepplewhite beneath her, half tumbling her onto the seat.

"Except for the cracked coach wheel, you had a pleasant journey I trust?" he asked.

"Yes, indeed. Very pleasant, but quite fatiguing," Abigail hinted. She would have felt much more at ease if Mr. Harding would only light somewhere instead of pacing up and down before her like a caged beast. The fringes on his very odd trousers shimmied with every movement he made. It was most distracting.

"I see you are admiring my breeches," he said.

"No, most certainly not!" Abigail cried, outraged by the mere suggestion of such a thing.

"I adopted the style from a fur trapper I met once. It's a very practical design. You notice these fringes?" He thrust one muscular leg forward for her inspection.

"Uh—er—yes," Abigail stammered, fearing she was noticing far too much.

"These fringes help to drain off the water when you get caught in the rain. That way a man doesn't end up wandering around in soaking buckskins."

"How—how interesting," Abigail said faintly, assailed by a vision of how Nate Harding would look in a pair of wet, clinging breeches. Doing her best to dispel the disturbing idea, she groped inside her reticule for her fan, then remembered with regret she had packed them all. But who would have ever expected it to be so warm in a drawing room this time of year?

"I suppose you don't find my attire very fashionable?" he prodded. "But I assure you, it does quite well in the wilds of Philadelphia. Just the thing for fighting off legions of bloodthirsty Indians on my way to market in the morning."

"Indeed?" Abigail said. Mr. Harding was clearly one of those gentlemen who would feed one as many Banbury tales as possible if allowed to do so. "I thought most of the Indians in America reside west of the Ohio these days."

He smiled, looking not in the least abashed to be caught out in his fabrication.

"Ah, the lady must read," he drawled.

"It is an accomplishment usually required in a governess, Mr. Harding."

"I am a little more curious about the nature of your other accomplishments, Mistress Abigail."

Abigail was relieved to discuss anything other than his breeches, but she thought she sensed an edge in his voice, a faint hint of challenge perhaps?

31

She longed to point out to him that most Englishmen rarely troubled themselves over the accomplishments of a governess. That was usually left to
the province of a wife or mother. Besides, she had
already been over her qualifications with Lady
Harding.

Still as master of this house, Mr. Harding's in-
quiries could not be so easily dismissed. He was not
the raw schoolboy she had thought he would be.

She sighed. "What is it you wish to know about
me, Mr. Harding? I can supply you with any references you desire if—"

"No, Nell already showed me those," he interrupted. "They were very impressive."

"Nell?"

"Lady Helen. My stepmother."

"Oh. I am afraid that I thought—"

"That Nell was my mother? No, much better
than that. She has always been my friend."

"I see," Abigail said, though she didn't. What
very odd relationships these Americans must have
with one another. It sounded rather disrespectful
the way Mr. Harding referred to Lady Harding, yet
he obviously spoke with a great deal of warmth and
affection.

"I am the product of my father's first marriage,
Mistress Abigail," he said.

That at least explained why Mr. Harding was so
much older and so different in appearance from his
sisters.

He continued, "My mother was the only daughter of Hans Sebastian Buckmeister. Perhaps even
over here you have heard of him? He was a Colonel,
a hero of our great war."

"Great war? Oh, you mean your revolution."

"I mean our war for independence." This was pronounced with a certain amount of fierceness.

Was it her imagination, Abigail wondered, or was she starting to detect the presence of a chip upon Mr. Harding's broad American shoulder?

"Er, yes," she agreed, attempting to steer the conversation back into safer channels. "If you find no fault with my references, Mr. Harding, exactly what questions do you have regarding my teaching abilities?"

He propped one boot up on a footstool and leaned forward, resting one arm upon his knee in an aggressive stance. She resisted the impulse to shrink back and allow herself to be disconcerted by any male who was all muscle and intimidation.

"I want to know," he demanded, "exactly what you mean to teach my sisters."

"Well, I—"

"They have already been to a cursed fine school in Philadelphia."

"I know that, sir. I have only been engaged by Lady Harding to remedy some of the defects in their education."

"Defects?" he scowled, and Abigail realized that had been a poor choice of word.

"To teach them some of the things they could not possibly have learned in America," she amended.

"She as?"

Such as how to recognize a Queen Anne period piece, and not to put their dusty boots on the footstool, and not to perform tasks that should have been left to the servants. And definitely not to discuss how a man should weatherproof his breeches!

Abigail managed to quell these thoughts, framing a more civil reply. "I can acquaint Louisa and

Clarice with their English heritage, with our ways and customs, prepare them for their first Season in London."

"How?" Mr. Harding no longer made any effort to disguise his contempt. "By teaching them fancy ways to curtsy and how to flirt with a fan?"

"No, Mr. Harding. I have never made a study of flirting."

"Comes to you naturally, does it?"

Not half so naturally as she was prepared to wager it came to him. Once more Abigail swallowed a retort and maintained her calm tone.

"I teach nothing that is frivolous, sir," she said. "My accomplishments include French, drawing, needlework, music, in short everything a lady should know. I am also qualified to instruct in mathematics, literature, geography—"

"Geography would be good," he interpolated.

"—*and* history."

His eyes narrowed a little at that. "What sort of history? Ancient or recent?"

"Both."

"Yours or ours, Mistress Abigail?"

"I beg your pardon?"

"The British version or the American?" he asked impatiently.

"I thought there was only one version."

"There is—the tale of how bold, brave men like my grandfather fought to throw off the yoke of tyranny, to become a nation of free men."

"I will admit that the American colonies did have some grievances against our king."

"How generous of you!"

"But your countrymen might have found a more civilized means of redress than destroying crown property and attacking poor tax collectors who were only attempting to do their duty."

"Violence begets violence, Mistress Prentiss. What about the British practice of unlawfully invading colonists' homes, of breaking up peaceful assemblies?"

"Violence is never the solution to anything, sir," Abigail said hotly, only to break off, realizing the absurdity of the conversation. She forced a smile to her lips. "This is foolish, Mr. Harding. We are quarreling about events that took place when we were both in leading strings. The differences between our two countries are well in the past."

"Are they? Obviously you haven't been reading the papers lately, ma'am. Or maybe they don't publish such information in your *London Post* about how American seamen are regularly being kidnapped by the British."

"Well, you need not look so accusingly at me, Mr. Harding. I haven't got them! You may search my trunks if you like."

The grim expression that hardened his features softened a little. "I don't think that will be necessary."

Abigail rose to her feet, feeling more exhausted by these past fifteen minutes than her entire bone-rattling journey from London. "If you don't mind, Mr. Harding, I am really very tired. Perhaps the rest of this discussion could keep for another time. I am beginning to feel like some poor heretic summoned to face the grand inquisitor."

He smiled at that. "I am sorry, Mistress Prentiss. I tend to get carried away sometimes. I suppose I can hold my stake and pile of kindling in abeyance for a while."

The dreadful thing was Abigail feared he was only half jesting. She had no difficulty imagining Nathaniel Harding lighting the flames beneath her feet and with no more than the fire in his eyes.

He strode to the door and shouted for Mrs. Bridges. Abigail rolled her eyes. Was Mr. Harding totally unacquainted with the fact that he had footmen to perform such errands as fetching the housekeeper and thus save the master of the house from having to bellow his lungs out?

Mrs. Bridges appeared in short order. She was a plump, stately woman whose starched appearance Abigail immediately approved. The housekeeper's expression remained quite wooden when once more Mr. Harding moved to assume the burden of Abigail's trunk. Abigail looked the other way herself, realizing by this time that remonstrating with Mr. Harding would be a pointless exercise.

As the three of them climbed the staircase to the upper floor, Mrs. Bridges said, "There is a very pleasant chamber on the third story, miss, where I believe the last governess to come to this house resided."

"That sounds quite satisfactory, Mrs. Bridges," Abigail began, when she was interrupted by Mr. Harding's growl.

"Up under the roof? It will be as cold and drafty as the devil. No, ma'am, there are plenty of fine rooms on this floor."

Still balancing the chest, he shoved open the door of the nearest one and peered inside. "This one is nice," he pronounced. He shouldered his way inside and plunked down the trunk.

Abigail crept to the threshold and looked in herself. Nice? It was practically a state chamber, all ivory and gilt with a lofty ceiling and a massive four-poster bed. The costly silk hangings were as vivid blue as Mr. Harding's eyes.

Abigail sensed Mrs. Bridges at her side, the woman gone rigid with disapproval. Abigail realized that nothing could be more damaging to her position here than if the other servants got the notion that the new governess was too uppity, seeking to be above her station.

Drawing in a deep breath, Abigail said, "Mr. Harding, this simply will not do."

The man was already flinging open curtains, but he turned to frown at her. "What's wrong with it?"

"This is obviously meant to be one of the guest bedchambers."

"So? I don't plan on doing any entertaining. And even if I did, this place is riddled with other bedchambers. We've got more rooms here than in the White House that was built for our president in Washington."

"That may well be," Abigail said with as much patience as though she were addressing a recalcitrant child. "But this sort of chamber was never intended for the governess." She directed an appealing smile toward the housekeeper. "I am sure the room you mentioned on the third floor will suit me better."

"I am not hauling that blasted trunk up another flight of stairs," Mr. Harding said.

"I will take it up myself if I have to." Bending over, Abigail began tugging at the handle, scooting it across the carpet.

She started when Mr. Harding jammed his foot on top of the trunk, preventing her from moving it any farther. He glared down at her.

"Are you always this difficult, ma'am? Small wonder you've had so many different places of employment."

Abigail straightened, the heat in her cheeks not so much from her recent exertions as her sudden flare of temper. "How dare you! My changing situations so often has had nothing to do with my performance as a governess. I have never had one complaint lodged against me. Not one!"

"You are about to receive your first if you don't do as I tell you, Mistress Abigail."

"The proper way to address me is *Miss Prentiss*."

His eyes flashed dangerously. "Let's get one thing clear. You are here because Helen thinks my sisters need you. But I do not require any Englishwoman giving me orders under my own roof. One of the things my ancestors fought for was freedom, *Mistress Abigail*."

"And let me make one thing clear to you, Mr. Harding, I did not come here to fight the revolutionary war all over again."

"Good!" he said. "You wouldn't win."

Crooking his fingers beneath her chin, he tipped up her head to meet his gaze. The boldness of the gesture, the intimacy of it, left Abigail momentarily too stunned to react.

His eyes were like blue steel, full of fire and challenge and the simmering of some other more powerful emotion. Abigail had the oddest notion that if Mrs. Bridges had not been present, Mr. Harding might have leaned forward and taken Abigail's lips in a long, hard kiss. Her heart hammered in her chest, and she felt breathless.

No, she had to be imagining things. Kiss her? Mr. Harding looked far more likely to strangle her.

He said tersely, "This bedchamber will be yours for the duration of your stay at Ashdown Manor. Do I make myself plain, ma'am?"

Abigail recovered enough presence of mind to thrust his hand away. "Perfectly, sir," she snapped.

Pivoting on his heel, Mr. Harding stalked past Mrs. Bridges, who had stood as still as a bedpost throughout the entire exchange. When Mr. Harding had gone, Abigail thought she glimpsed a hint of sympathy in the woman's eyes, but it was gone in a flash, shuttered away behind the housekeeper's stony expression.

"I'll send Nancy up directly to air the room and bring you some water for washing, miss," she said.

Abigail wanted to tell the woman not to bother. Abigail was not staying under the roof of the arrogant Mr. Harding another minute.

But reason always ruled Abigail even during those rare times she lost her temper. "Yes, thank you, Mrs. Bridges," she heard herself reply. "That would be most kind."

Only after the housekeeper had quit the room, did Abigail allow herself to feel how badly shaken she was by the recent contretemps with Mr. Harding. She pressed her hands to her heated face. It was as though she could still feel the rough warm contact of his fingers beneath her chin.

As her calm returned, she realized she had been wise to hold her tongue. Of course, she was going nowhere. How disappointed Lady Harding and her daughters would be if they returned home to discover that Miss Prentiss had fled.

And how disappointed Miss Prentiss would be in herself. In her time, she had faced the wrath and hauteur of both dukes and duchesses, even a rear admiral. She was hardly going to allow herself to be driven off by one belligerent Yankee.

No! Abigail resolved. She had come here to accomplish one thing, to turn the misses Hardings into proper, elegant English ladies, acceptable to the *ton*. And she would manage to do it in spite of their brother and his boorish behavior. That infernal man could clearly ruin his sisters' first Season if he were permitted to do so. Mr. Nathaniel Harding could use a few lessons in manners himself, although thank God, Abigail thought fervently, teaching him was not her job.

She knew what her task was, and as long as she confined herself to that, she would do just fine here at Ashdown Manor. As though to reassure herself, Abigail stalked over to her trunk and unearthed the small sampler she always took with her wherever she went. As a reminder . . .

Lifting the wooden frame up into the light, she gazed down at the neatly embroidered letters.

Keep within compass, and you shall be sure to avoid many troubles that others endure.

It was the motto by which Abigail Prentiss governed her life. Keeping within compass, knowing one's place in the world and being satisfied with it, maintaining one's standards of proper behavior, never straying beyond one's boundaries—that was the key to true contentment.

Only once had she ever strayed from that precept, and it had nearly been her ruin. Most certainly, it had brought her nothing but heartbreak.

Never again, Abigail thought, hugging the wooden frame to her like a precious talisman. She would find a place to display it at once. She had the feeling she might need the reminder more often than usual with the disconcerting Mr. Harding about.

One thing was certain. She would not permit him to ruffle her equanimity or allow him to make her lose her temper again. Such display of emotion was not to be tolerated in a truly superior governess.

Walking briskly across the room, Abigail took down an indifferent watercolor situated on the far wall. She hung her sampler in its place, and was striving to make sure the frame was straight when she chanced to glance out the window.

A movement on the drive below caught her eye, Mr. Harding vaulting on the back of a large roan gelding. At least the man was a little more respectably dressed. He had donned a tailcoat, but he wore no hat. The sun glinted gold off his windblown mane of hair.

Abigail would never know what mischance caused him to look up. It was almost as though he sensed her presence at the window. He gave her a mocking smile, and raised one of his gloves by way of salute before wheeling his horse around and galloping off across the lawn.

Abigail's lips thinned. It was almost as if the infernal man had just waved a gauntlet at her.

Keep within compass, Abigail, she reminded herself, exhaling a fierce sigh. Of course, *she* would do so.

But could any man as rough-and-ready as Nate Harding be trusted to do the same?

Chapter 3

Much to Abigail's relief, she saw no more of Mr. Harding that evening. Nor did the gentleman put in an appearance at breakfast the following morning. Lady Harding and her daughters had arrived home late last night, and by the time Abigail was conducted into their presence, she was restored to her state of customary equanimity. The young ladies' warm and delighted welcome did much to soothe Abigail's feelings, ruffled from her encounter with Mr. Harding.

Lady Harding was just as Abigail had remembered her from their interviews in London, a gentle, sympathetic sort of woman. Abigail meant to speak to her at first opportunity about overriding Mr. Harding's peremptory orders and having Abigail moved to a bedchamber more suitable for a governess.

In the meantime, Abigail briskly adjourned to the small parlor on the second floor, which had been given over to her use for a classroom. While two of the footmen moved the pianoforte into the room, Abigail began unpacking her things; a handsome globe that had been a present from one of her previous employers, the crusty Admiral Lewes, her easel and watercolors, and her assortment of books.

Any lingering doubts she might have had about accepting the position at Ashdown Manor were soon dispelled by the enthusiastic way her new charges pitched in to help her. Louisa and Clarice exclaimed with delight as each of Abigail's treasures emerged from her trunk, from her well-loved sheets of music to her copies of *La Belle Assemblée* depicting the latest fashions from France.

Louisa discovered Abigail's map of London, and spread it out upon the oak worktable. She pored over it, saying, "We saw so little of the city when we were there last month, Miss Prentiss. We only stayed a fortnight, and Mama was feeling poorly." Louisa tapped her finger at one spot on the map. "Is that St. James Street? Is it true what we have heard, that no lady should ever be seen walking or riding there alone?"

"Perfectly true," Abigail replied.

"But why ever not?"

"I expect it is because all the gentlemen's clubs are located there," Clarice said in that solemn way of hers, peering over her sister's shoulder. "All the men would be likely to ogle and stare at us."

"I thought that was the idea," Louisa said with a wicked wag of her eyebrows.

Abigail frowned. It was obvious she was going to have trouble with that one. The child was lively and pert, her countenance full of fire and animation. She quite cast poor Clarice into the shade, though oddly enough it was Clarice who possessed the greater perfection of feature and promised to be the real beauty of the family one day.

But Abigail set aside her apprehensions about Louisa for the moment. She kept a firm hand on her charges, but she never commenced any post by delivering lectures right off. Instead she joined the girls at the table, and allowed them to ply her with questions about the city where they would make their debut next spring.

Abigail was just beginning to explain to them about Almack's when she heard a sound from the hallway. A familiar masculine voice boomed out inquiring after the whereabouts of Miss Louisa and Clarice. Abigail tensed, realizing for the first time that she had been on tenterhooks all morning, listening for the sound of that voice.

But such behavior was absurd. It was not as if she could hope to avoid Mr. Harding forever. She heard him receive a muffled reply to his inquiry, and presently there came a brisk rap at the parlor door. By the time it swung open, Abigail had managed to compose herself.

Mr. Harding loomed large in the doorway, obviously fresh from his morning's ride, his waves of ash blond hair appearing to have caught the sun, his greatcoat scented with the smell of outdoors.

"Good morrow, ladies," he said pleasantly. "Mistress Prentiss." He acknowledged Abigail with a brief bow.

Abigail did not know quite what she had expected from him after their quarrel of yesterday. Perhaps a frigid reserve to match her own, or at least he might have the grace to seem a little apologetic. She had *not* expected him to look so annoyingly cheerful.

"At your lessons already, ma'am?" he asked. "I

see you waste little time. I admire that in a woman."

"Th-thank you," Abigail said, thrown off balance by the unlooked-for compliment. What was it about the man, she wondered? He had to but enter a room to give one the breathless sensation of being assailed by a strong, powerful wind.

"Nate," Louisa called out eagerly. "Miss Prentiss has been teaching us all about London."

"Don't tell me. Let me guess," he drawled. "It isn't Philadelphia."

Louisa crinkled her nose at him. "Don't be so teasing, Nate. Miss Prentiss has this most wonderful map. Do but come and look."

"I am afraid I am not prepared for any geography lessons this morning. I only came because I finished my business with the steward early, and I wondered if you girls wished to go riding with me."

Clarice glanced up at her older brother, open adoration in her dove gray eyes. "Oh, Nate, I would love to—"

"But we are in the middle of a lesson." Louisa pouted. "Miss Prentiss was just explaining to us about Almack's, this place where they have these wonderfully fashionable balls. I want to hear the rest."

"It will keep for another time, Louisa," Abigail began.

"Oh, no, I have no wish to interfere, ma'am. Finish your discussion." Mr. Harding settled himself upon the threshold, leaning one broad shoulder against the doorjamb. "Don't mind me. I can wait."

Don't mind him? How was one not supposed to mind six feet of overpowering male hovering in one's doorway? But Mr. Harding appeared quite content where he was, raising a red rose to his nostrils to sniff at the sweet fragrance. It was the first that Abigail noticed he had the flower, and she found the sight of the delicate blossom cupped in his strong, tanned fingers somehow very distracting.

She didn't realize she was staring until she felt Louisa's impatient tug on her sleeve. Doing her best to ignore Mr. Harding, she turned her attention back to the map.

"Now let me see. Yes, Almack's . . . The assembly rooms are here in King Street, and no one is ever permitted to enter without a rose—I mean a voucher. But it is very important to a lady's social success to be seen there of a Wednesday evening."

"Hold one moment," Mr. Harding called out. "Let me see if I understand this correctly."

Abigail glanced up to see his brow furrowed in the hint of a frown. He absently whisked the petals of the rose across the full curve of his lower lip in a way that caused an inexplicable quiver to shoot through Abigail.

"It's important to go to this fancy ball," he mused. "But you can't get in without a ticket?"

"One must first have a voucher to be allowed to purchase a ticket, Mr. Harding."

"And just how much are these *vouchers* going to cost me?"

"Oh, Nate, really!" Louisa exclaimed in mortified accents.

"The cost of the ticket is a mere trifle, but the vouchers come a little more dear," Abigail explained patiently. "To be admitted to Almack's membership list, one must first obtain the approval of the seven noble ladies who sponsor the assemblies."

"I see. Well, that could prove a problem for me and my sisters, ma'am. Americans aren't accustomed to truckling to anyone."

"No one is asking you to truckle, Mr. Harding. Breeding, elegance, and courtesy are what is required, and if you—" Drawing a deep breath, Abigail broke off, sensing that the conversation was drifting into dangerous waters. She could scarce believe it. Mr. Harding had not been in the same room above ten minutes, and she was already close to quarreling with him again. And to add to her irritation, she began to suspect Mr. Harding actually enjoyed baiting her.

Turning aside, Abigail began to roll up the map. "That is enough about Almack's and London for now, ladies. We will set up a schedule for our studies as soon as I am more properly settled in."

Clarice meekly accepted this, but Louisa glared at her brother. "Now look what you've gone and done, Nate. You've managed to upset Miss Prentiss already."

"Why? What did I do?" Mr. Harding asked in a voice of pained astonishment. But Louisa ignored him, placing one hand placatingly on Abigail's arm.

"You mustn't mind Nate's teasing, truly. I expect he is just cross because he has not managed to turn you up sweet as he does with most women."

"Louisa!" her brother growled a warning.

"It's true," Clarice added with gentle pride. "Back home Nate had most of the young ladies in Philadelphia chasing after him."

Abigail felt a surge of heat steal into her cheeks.

She said sternly, "In England, Miss Clarice, ladies don't chase after gentlemen."

"Set traps for them, do you, ma'am?" Mr. Harding asked.

Abigail finished rolling the map with a final sharp snap. "I think perhaps all of you had best prepare for your ride. It is likely to rain soon."

"Nonsense. There isn't a cloud in the sky."

Abigail pursed her lips. Did the man propose to argue with her about everything?

"I can't imagine why you want us to go riding anyway, Nate," Louisa said. "You've never thought of it before. You always say Clarice and I are cursed nuisances."

"So are my mules back home. But even nuisances need to be exercised."

"Oh, you—" Louisa sputtered, pulling a face at him. Abigail made a mental note to remind her pupil that young ladies did not thrust their tongues out at gentlemen. Although in Mr. Harding's case, Abigail could understand the temptation.

"Brat!" he said.

"Churl!" Louisa shot back.

"Baggage!"

"Ruffian!"

Abigail might have been appalled by this exchange if she had not sensed the vein of good humor beneath it. Mr. Harding chased both Louisa and Clarice off to change into their riding habits amid a barrage of playful threats, tweaking of curls, and much laughter.

One could almost feel the degree of warmth and affection that existed between him and his sisters. It stood in marked contrast to the stiff, unloving relationship Abigail had known with her own brother.

She scarce realized with what degree of wistfulness she watched this little scene until the girls had vanished out the door. When Mr. Harding turned back abruptly and caught her staring, Abigail made haste to bend over the trunk, pretending to be absorbed in unpacking her books.

She hoped that he would now take his leave as well. But he didn't. To her dismay, she heard the creak of his boots as he crossed the room to stand behind her.

After a brief hesitation, he cleared his throat. "We appear to have gotten off on a very bad footing, Mistress Abigail."

"It is of no consequence, Mr. Harding. As you so aptly pointed out to me yesterday, I am not to be your governess."

"That doesn't mean we have to be at daggers drawn." He gave a rueful sigh. "There just seems to be something about you that brings out the schoolboy in me. I keep getting these devilish urges to tie knots in your bonnet strings and slip snakes among your things."

Abigail jerked back from her trunk at once, peering suspiciously inside.

"Oh, don't worry. I haven't done so . . . *yet*."

Flooded with relief, Abigail relaxed, but she said, "It would do you very little good if you had, Mr. Harding. When I became a governess, I anticipated such pranks, and I trained myself to handle snakes, toads, and sundry other slimy creatures with complete aplomb."

"Did you?" His delighted chuckle sounded rich

and warm. "Good for you, ma'am." After a pause, he asked, "Did you sleep well last night?"

"Why do you ask? Did you tuck some mice beneath my coverlets?"

"No, ma'am. After our—er—disagreement over your chamber, I simply wondered how you had fared."

"I fared well enough, Mr. Harding."

"Ah, then I was right about you having that bedchamber."

"Comfort was never the issue, sir. Perhaps I did not make myself clear. I did not mean to seem ungracious when I tried to refuse—"

"Good. Then I accept your apology."

"My apology!" Abigail straightened to face him with an outraged gasp. But she was totally disarmed by the unexpected twinkle in his blue eyes, the charm of his smile. How was it possible that a man of such rugged features could actually have dimples?

"Truce, Mistress Abigail?" he asked, holding out the rose to her.

Abigail stared at the flower, uncomprehending.

"Take it," he urged. "When I passed through the garden, I plucked it just for you."

When she made no move to accept it, he teased, "What is wrong? Governesses don't approve of roses either?"

"Of course not. Governesses, I—I mean I am very fond of roses, but—"

"Then pray, accept this one and say 'thank you kindly, sir.' Especially after I risked life and limb to get it for you. Look." He displayed a tiny scratch on the pad of his thumb, presumably made by a thorn.

"The rose reminded me of you. Beautiful, but it bites."

"Mr. Harding!" Abigail protested, shaking her head.

"Take it," he insisted more gruffly this time. He caught her hand and cupped it about the stem of the flower. "And don't worry. I shaved off all the thorns with my jackknife."

Abigail scarce knew when she had been at such a loss for words. She did not comprehend why such a simple gesture should overwhelm her so. Perhaps because it had been a long time since a gentleman had presented her with a flower. Not since the fleeting days of her girlhood.

The days of her girlhood. Both the thought and the memory brought an ache to her heart. She suddenly had a clear image of herself at seventeen, a nervous young governess trying to maintain order among the Duke of Rivington's small daughters in the nursery. One of the duke's younger sons had appeared in the doorway, smiling at her with great sympathy. Lord Eliot Windom had been not much older than she, a handsome gentleman, quiet and shy. He had welcomed her to the house with a nose-gay of violets, and she had accepted it with trembling hands, her eyes meeting his across the bouquet. Thus had the folly begun. . . .

The memory paled as she stared down at Mr. Harding's single rose. She was a good deal older and wiser now, wise enough to know she should have refused the flowers in a manner of firm politeness. But what did she have to fear in this instance? Mr. Harding's brusque offhand gesture was worlds different from what Lord Eliot's tender offering had been. Coming from a man like Nate

Harding, the gift of a rose could be no more than a harmless whim.

Indeed, he seemed to have forgotten about both the flower and herself already as he began unpacking her books, grimacing at the titles as he stacked them on the table. *"History of British Monarchs. William the Conqueror. Manners and Morals for Well-Bred Young Ladies.* Don't you have any good books, Mistress—" He stopped abruptly as he unearthed a slender pamphlet. *"The Rights of Man."* He quirked one brow at her. "*You* read Thomas Paine?"

"Certainly. Does that so astonish you, sir? You forget that Mr. Paine was one of my countrymen before he became one of yours. Whether you credit it or not, Mr. Harding, we English also take an interest in human rights and liberties. This is the land of Magna Carta."

"Also the land of privilege, kings, princes, and dukes."

"At least we hold no slaves over here."

"We don't have slaves in Philadelphia either." But Mr. Harding's cheeks reddened slightly. "I will admit that the practice of slavery is my country's burning shame. It is an evil that I pray will one day be eradicated, and then we will truly have freedom for all in America."

He looked so troubled that Abigail almost regretted having taunted him with his country's hypocrisy, but she could not resist adding, "Freedom for all, Mr. Harding? Including the ladies?"

He met her challenge with his glinting smile.

"Aye, Mistress Abigail. It might astound you to know that I would indeed be an advocate for more rights for ladies, even including the right to vote."

Abigail gaped at him.

He laughed. "I see I have managed to shock even you with such a radical notion."

"You have indeed, sir. Women voting is something I have never considered. I have observed my sister Jane since her marriage. She has not had an opinion to call her own, and I fear many women are like her. They would only vote as their husbands told them to."

"I can't imagine any man telling you what to do, Mistress Abigail. Has any ever been foolhardy enough to make that attempt?"

Besides Mr. Harding himself? Abigail thought repressing a smile. But his words stirred the coals of another memory, herself in the Duke of Rivington's study, bidding farewell to Lord Eliot Windom, blinking back her tears.

"You must agree with me, my lord," she had whispered. "Considering the circumstances, my going away would be the wisest, most sensible thing."

And yet she had been unable to keep from hoping that he would find the strength, the courage to defy both his parents and Abigail's common sense. To say her nay, to forbid her to go . . .

Realizing that Mr. Harding still awaited an answer to his question, Abigail sighed.

"No, Mr. Harding," she said sadly. "There has never been any man who attempted to interfere with the course of my life."

"Now, that's a great pity." The rough edges of his voice softened, his vivid blue eyes becoming almost gentle.

Abigail found herself uncomfortable with the turn of the conversation. Pacing a few steps away from him, she avoided his gaze by burying her nose in the sweet fragrant petals of the rose.

"And now that I have gratified your curiosity, Mr. Harding," she said, "perhaps I might be permitted a question of my own."

He looked a little wary, but he replied, "Ask away, Mistress Prentiss. Just bear in mind, I am, after all, only a boorish Yankee. If I don't like the question, I may tell you to go be hanged."

"This 'Yankee' business is precisely what I wished to ask you about. Your father was an English lord. You, yourself are now in possession of a handsome English country estate. Surely that makes you—"

"An Englishman? Never say so, Mistress Prentiss. I'd as soon be called a jackanapes. Make no mistake, ma'am. I was born and bred an American, and an American I will always be. I promised my late father to suffer the hospitality of your country for the course of the year. But come next July, I will be celebrating Independence Day back in Philadelphia."

Abigail regarded him in astonishment. "But your lands, your inheritance? What will you do with Ashdown Manor?"

He hunched his shoulders in a dismissive shrug that Abigail found appalling. This comfortable estate that he seemed to take so lightly would have been highly prized by any of her own countrymen. What a difference the inheritance of such lands would have made in her own life.

"I don't precisely know what I'll do with Ashdown Manor," he said. "It is not entailed, so I suppose I could sell it or simply let it out. The estate fairly runs itself. I never met my late uncle, but he must have been a shrewd man. He placed the management of his lands in good hands. I ride out with Mr. Bell, the steward, upon occasion. He insists upon deferring to me on estate questions, but hellfire! I was never much of a farmer, not even back in Pennsylvania."

Nate dragged his hand back through his shagged mane of blond hair, disordering it further. The gesture was rife with restlessness and frustration. "I'm not cut out to play lord of the manor either. There simply isn't enough for me to do here. Back home, I was accustomed to pursuing a variety of pursuits, reading law, designing buildings, helping my uncle run the shipyard." He glanced defensively at Abigail. "All occupations that over here are considered to be beneath the notice of a gentleman."

"You are fortunate to have such choices, sir," she said. "And yes, you are correct. The sons of English noblemen are usually restricted to careers in either the military or the clergy."

"And if a poor fellow has no aptitude for either, ma'am? Then he is left in rather a bad way, such as my own father. I suppose you knew that my father was considered the black sheep of the noble Harding family?" he asked somewhat bitterly.

"No, I didn't, but I don't think that you should speak of—" Abigail started to demur.

"Oh, don't look so alarmed, ma'am. I'm not about to regale you with any great scandal. My father's sins were very tame. While he was posted in the wilds of America, he had the effrontery to both sell out of his commission in the British army and to marry a Pennsylvania farmer's daughter. His family never forgave him, and he became a permanent exile."

Mr. Harding's harsh expression softened. "I suppose you could say that my father gave up his country for the woman he loved. Do you not find that romantic, Mistress Prentiss?"

"It sounds more like the beginnings of a tragedy."

"Nothing so dramatic. I believe my father rested content enough while my mother lived. He even survived and managed to remain neutral during the War of Independence. But my mother perished of the typhus when I was eleven. My father was lost for a time, until he found and wed Nell. She was a British diplomat's daughter, and my father's family actually approved the match. He was finally forgiven, but he made no effort to return to England, though I am convinced he was never truly happy in Pennsylvania."

Any more than you are happy here, Abigail thought as she studied Mr. Harding's somber expression. Shadows pooled in his eyes, and there was a taut set to the mouth that she guessed was usually reserved for good humor and laughter.

She suddenly found herself intrigued by this man who seemed so rough-hewn, stubborn, even a little crude. Beneath the brash exterior, she sensed, lurked a man of greater depth of feeling, of sensitivity than she had supposed. She longed to know more about Nate Harding, about his family.

Abigail brought herself up short, both disconcerted and dismayed by the direction of her own thoughts. This was not within her province as governess. She had no business seeking to know anything of Nate Harding's personal life.

Keep within compass she reminded herself severely.

Depositing the rose he had given her atop the

pile of books, she faced him with what she hoped was a distant and dismissive smile.

"Goodness, Mr. Harding. How long I have kept you here talking. You had best make haste down to the stables, or I fear your sisters will wax quite impatient."

The sound of her voice snapped Mr. Harding out of whatever unhappy thoughts absorbed him. "What—oh yes, if I keep Louisa waiting, there will be the devil to pay. She's a pert wench. You'll have much ado to keep the reins pulled in on her, Mistress Abigail. And speaking of reins, we should all be pleased if you would join us on our ride. There is a pretty little mare down in the stables that I am certain would just suit you."

For a moment, Abigail was flooded with remembrance of how it felt to go galloping across an open field, her hair blowing free in the wind. But that was a pleasure, like so many others, that belonged to her past.

"I am afraid I am a very indifferent rider, Mr. Harding," she lied. "I thank you for the invitation, but as you can see, I have much to do here if I am to commence your sisters' lessons in earnest."

Her refusal clearly disappointed Mr. Harding, and he looked prepared to give her an argument. He was not a man who easily took no for an answer. But with great effort, Abigail fancied, he restrained himself.

"Very well," he sighed. "I will hold you excused . . . this time. I am glad we had opportunity for this talk. I trust now we are at peace with one another?"

He held out his hand, and she had no choice but

to take it. Her slender fingers seemed swallowed up in the strength and heat of his grasp.

"Certainly, Mr. Harding," she managed to reply. "I never desired to be at war with you."

"How odd. I think that's the same thing the lobsterbacks said before they marched on Lexington."

His quip surprised a chuckle out of her. But the next instant the laughter stilled in her throat as he raised her hand to his lips. His blue eyes seemed to hold her captive as he pressed a warm and lingering kiss to her fingertips.

"You are big on hand kissing over here, are you not?" he asked. "This is the way I believe it is done."

"Not—not quite, Mr. Harding," Abigail said, her pulse quickening. She snatched her hand from his grasp. "Usually the gesture is—is a mere formality, a brush of the lips, something very—very impersonal."

His lips crooked into a slow, seductive smile. "Ah, Mistress Abigail. Only you British could ever believe that a kiss could be impersonal."

Looking highly amused, he sketched her a quick bow, backed across the threshold, and was gone. It was long minutes after Mr. Harding had left before Abigail became aware that she was standing like a stock. She was still clutching her own hand, and her fingers were trembling.

She drew in a steadying breath, and her glance fell upon the flower that she abandoned on top of the book stack. She stiffened with sudden alarm.

Was it just her imagination or did Mr. Harding's gift of a rose seem no longer so careless a gesture?

That evening, Nate whistled cheerfully as he dressed for dinner, taking more care with the arrangement of his neck cloth than was his custom. For perhaps the first time since he had set foot in this accursed stuffy English manor, the evening that stretched out ahead of him did not look quite so long and dull.

His good humor had a great deal to do with the fact he had succeeded in coaxing a genuine smile from the stone-faced Miss Prentiss. He had even made her laugh, and he found he liked the light, musical sound. It was a pleasant discovery to make about a woman whom he had been dead certain possessed no sense of humor.

He was willing to concede it might be partly his fault that he had gotten off to such a bad start with the new governess. He had teased her a little, but then she had stepped down from that carriage with her perfect nose thrust into the air.

And condescending in the bargain! She had not been in the house above an hour before she was giving him hints on how to conduct himself, telling him what was proper, even attempting to instruct him in the history of his own country.

Nate frowned a little at the memory as he padded about his bedchamber, struggling into a navy blue frock coat. But despite her contrary views, he was forced to admit the lady was intelligent. Any woman who read Paine could not be totally lacking in sense.

Nate looked forward to having someone at the dinner table capable of holding a real conversation, someone who would match him in wit. Nell and Clarice meekly agreed with everything that he said. As for Louisa, the girl didn't argue. She just bickered. He anticipated some lively debate from

Abigail, the stimulating kind he had not known since his last visit to a Philadelphia coffeehouse.

Presenting her with that rose had been a good notion. He'd only sought to make peace because he feared he might have gone too far yesterday. One couldn't have the new governess heading back for London in a state of high dudgeon. He would have never heard the end of it from Louisa and Clarice.

But by the time he had pressed the flower into Abigail's hand, he was glad he'd done it for the lady's own sake. She had looked so adorably flustered. He had glimpsed something in her eyes then, something sweet, achingly vulnerable, and womanly. And he wondered what the devil was the matter with all the men in this country. Here was a perfectly lovely lady being permitted to grow staid and old long before her time.

What Mistress Abby clearly needed was a bit of mild flirtation. And he was just the man to provide it, Nate thought with a grin, as he sank down on the edge of his bed to ease on his shoes. It had been a long time since he had enjoyed the company of a pretty woman.

The clock chiming upon the mantel reminded Nate of the lateness of the hour. Hastily he finished dressing. Smoothing back his hair, he took one final satisfied glance at himself in the mirror before bolting out of the bedchamber. Whistling cheerfully, he descended to the crimson drawing room where it had become the family's habit to assemble before dinner.

Nate was astonished to hear the voices of the ladies drifting out into the hall. Usually he was the first one down, growling with impatience until his sisters finally put in an appearance. Hurrying forward, he managed to reach the drawing room door before the ubiquitous Andrew for once. The footman shot him a mildly reproachful glance and slunk away crestfallen.

Nate entered the room to receive a warm smile of welcome from his stepmother. Lady Helen was seated upon the settee, attired in her best black bombazine. Nate hated the color, but he liked the healthy glow he saw on Nell's face.

"Good evening, my dear," she said. "My, don't you look fine this evening."

Nate gave the front of his new tailcoat a self-conscious pat as he bent to plant a kiss on Nell's cheek. But it was not his stepmother's approbation he was looking for. Straightening, he glanced eagerly about the room for the rest of the ladies.

They were at the far end of the drawing room. Looking like a pair of gauzy white butterflies, Louisa and Clarice were practicing curtsies in front of the large gilt-trimmed mirror. Miss Prentiss watched them with an encouraging eye.

The lady was garbed in a stiff gray silk that Nate found most unappealing. But he was enough of a connoisseur of the female frame to detect the lush swell of breast, the trim waist, the delectable curve of hip beneath the somber-hued gown. Abigail was a handsome filly no matter how she might seek to disguise that fact.

Nate had no difficulty imagining the way her hair would ripple over her shoulders like dusky silk if she would ever release it from her too-tight chignon. And those eyes of hers, thick-fringed, brilliant green, magnificent! A woman could inspire a man to all manner of sweet folly with eyes like that if she knew how to use them properly.

But it was obvious Miss Prentiss didn't. As Nate approached, she fixed him with a chilling stare that held no hint of the laughter they had shared earlier that day.

"Good evening, Mistress Abigail," he said, offering her a tentative smile, a smile that was not returned.

"Sir." She dipped into a frigid curtsy.

Damnation! Had the rose he'd given her wilted already?

Before he could say anything more, Louisa bounded in between them. "You are finally here, Nate."

"It doesn't appear as though anyone has been languishing for my presence," Nate said. What was the matter with Abigail? After their talk this afternoon, he had expected to find the lady a little more friendly. But it seemed she had her nose in the air a few degrees higher than before.

"You have been missing all the interesting things Miss Prentiss has been telling us about how to go into dinner," Louisa said.

"What do you mean *how* to go in?" Nate asked, wrenching his eyes with great difficulty from Abigail's uncompromising profile. "You put one foot after the other."

"No, I mean the order in which one does it. As the eldest Miss Harding, I always get to go in first, ahead of Clarice."

"Unless I marry before you do," Clarice objected. "Then I shall have precedence."

"Unless I marry a duke, and you only marry a lord—"

"No one is marrying any dukes or lords," Nate snapped, losing patience with this nonsense. "And

I recollect a time when you two decided who arrived at the table first by who ran the fastest."

Clarice shot him a pained glance, and Louisa huffed. "You never seem to realize that we are quite grown up now, Nate. We are ladies, and it wouldn't hurt you to learn to behave like a gentleman. Tell me what you would do. If you were holding a dinner party and there was a countess and a duchess present, which one would you choose to escort into the dining room?"

"I would choose Mistress Prentiss," he replied.

"I beg your pardon, sir," Abigail said.

"I always have the wit to select the prettiest woman in the room." Nate was gratified to see a deep blush stain Abigail's cheeks, but she eyed him as sternly as though he were an errant schoolboy.

"No, Mr. Harding! You would have to choose the duchess even if she squinted and had warts."

"Nate would not mind, Miss Prentiss," Clarice spoke up. "He is ever so kind. At the dances back home, he always stood up with every lady in the room, even the plainest ones."

"That is because he is a shocking flirt." Louisa giggled. "Though, I admit even I was impressed when he asked Mary Turkeltaub to dance. No other man in the room would have done so."

Nate glared at his sister. "Miss Turkeltaub is a young lady of—of amiable disposition and a good dancer."

"And now she is as smitten with Nate as the rest of those silly girls back home."

Nate thought he was going to throttle Louisa if she didn't stop rattling on about his conquests in Philadelphia. Mistress Prentiss looked disapproving enough without his sister adding fuel to the fire.

Happily at that moment, Andrew stepped into the room to announce that dinner was served. Turning to Abigail, Nate said, "Since there are no duchesses present, ma'am, and you clearly outrank these two baggages"—he indicated his indignant sisters—"I believe I may safely assume I am escorting you into dinner."

"What about Mama?" Clarice asked, her brow furrowed in serious consideration. "Wouldn't she be considered of higher rank than Miss Prentiss?"

"A man has two arms, doesn't he?" Nate retorted. In a manner that brooked no argument, he attempted to secure Abigail's hand.

But she neatly sidestepped him. "You keep forgetting, sir. I am the governess, not a guest here. Now if you will excuse me, Mr. Harding, young ladies."

She strode briskly across the room and made a respectful curtsy to Lady Helen. "Good night, my lady."

The next instant Miss Prentiss whisked herself out of the door, leaving Nate dumbfounded.

Abigail breathed a sigh of relief as she slipped out of the drawing room. She had been preparing herself all day to face Mr. Harding with a chilling politeness, to demonstrate the proper decorum between a governess and the master of the house. As she headed for the staircase, she hoped that she had finally succeeded.

But the hope was short-lived. She had scarce reached the first landing when she heard a determined stride closing the distance behind her.

"Mistress Prentiss!"

Abigail winced. She should have known matters would not be settled so easily. Nothing with Mr. Harding ever was. Coming about slowly, she saw him standing at the foot of the stairs. Candlelight played over the powerful set of his shoulders, the hints of gold in his thick waves of hair, the hard contours of his face. One rugged hand rested gracefully atop the newel post, the other was placed at his hip in an aggressive stance that boded ill.

"Where are you going?" he asked.

"Why, to take my supper, sir."

"The dining parlor isn't upstairs."

"I know that. Mrs. Bridges is sending up a tray to my room."

"The devil she is!" His thick brows drew together in a mighty scowl. "Hellfire! Can't you plainly see that I—that is, my sisters wish you to dine with our family?"

"I have already explained to Clarice and Louisa the reasons why I cannot do so."

He sprinted up the stairs two at a time until he towered over Abigail on the landing, blocking her path to the second flight of steps.

"Then explain to me," he demanded.

If Mr. Harding had been a reasonable gentleman, a reasonable *English* gentleman, Abigail would not have to explain to him what should be painfully obvious. She expelled a long-suffering sigh.

"Governesses are not invited to the dining parlor, Mr. Harding. They usually take their meals in the schoolroom or occasionally with the housekeeper."

"Is that so? Well, we have different notions of hospitality where I come from, ma'am. Any visiting schoolmaster or schoolmistress is accorded a place of honor at the family table."

"That may do well enough in your country, sir. But this is not Philadelphia."

"How wonderful to live in a household full of women so well versed in geography. Now, will you kindly stop spouting nonsense, Mistress Abby, and come back down before everyone's dinner gets cold?"

Mistress Abby! Heat stung Abigail's cheeks. The man went quite too far.

"Mr. Harding! I do not seem to be making myself clear. I have never dined with the family in any of the noble houses where I served."

"This isn't a noble household, only a simple Yankee one. You have a choice, ma'am. You can come down to the dining parlor or else."

"Or else what?" Abigail said, meeting the challenge in his steely blue eyes.

"Or else I may be forced to carry you!"

Abigail's lips set in a mutinous line, daring him to try it. But when he advanced upon her in menacing fashion, she realized the ruffian was fully capable of executing his threat. Backing up against the landing wall, she felt a rush of apprehension, anger, and a strange, unsettling excitement.

"The truth is, Mistress Abby," he said, his eyes glinting down at her, "you are an infernal snob just like most Englishwomen. That's the real reason you don't wish to dine with us."

"How—how perfectly ridiculous," Abigail sputtered.

"I can't think that you can find any fault with Helen or the girls, so I expect it's me you keep turning your nose up at."

"I am sure I have never shown you any disrespect or said anything to make you think—"

"You don't have to. Your eyes say it for you. You've made it quite plain since we first met that you find me an intolerable barbarian."

"Your present behavior is hardly calculated to make me think otherwise," she said scornfully. "Are these the sort of rustic manners that won you so many hearts back in Philadelphia?"

Mr. Harding's face washed a full red, and his eyes narrowed ominously. As he pressed closer, Abigail knew a moment of real alarm. She was not certain whether he meant to fling her over his shoulder or strangle her. Or perhaps he had something entirely different in mind, his gaze fixed upon her mouth with a hot, angry intensity.

Abigail's heart skipped a beat. But she was too mortified and too stubborn to cry out for help. Just as she wondered if she was going to have to box his ears, Mr. Harding seemed to snap to his senses.

He flung himself away from her, growling, "Oh, the devil with it! Go on up to your room. You can eat on the roof for all I care."

"Thank you, sir." Though she was feeling strangely weak, Abigail skirted past him and paraded up the second stretch of stairs with injured dignity.

"But—" The sound of his voice stayed her once more. "If you persist in refusing to dine with my family, be warned, ma'am. The truce between us is over."

Abigail paused in midstep to regard him warily. "And just what does that mean, sir?"

"It means that if it is war you want, lady, I shall be happy to oblige you." An unholy smile crossed his face.

"Mr. Harding," Abigail protested stiffly, "I never desired—"

But the infernal man was already striding back down the stairs. Abigail watched his militant retreat with indignation and dismay.

If she wanted war, he would give it to her? Abigail could not imagine what devilish design such a remark portended. But she had a sinking feeling she would soon find out.

Chapter 4

The mist seemed to be everywhere, billowing at Abigail's feet, curling about her head, obscuring her vision. Raising her dueling pistol with grim determination, she stood back-to-back with Mr. Nate Harding, awaiting the signal to begin. But when she attempted to pace off her steps, the heavy fog weighted her boots, caused her pistol to vanish before her very eyes.

Whirling about, Abigail was taken aback to find Nate but inches away from her, grinning.

"Mr. Harding. This duel is not being conducted properly," she shouted. "Where are the seconds? And where is my pistol?"

He seized her by the shoulders. "Only you British could believe that dueling could be so impersonal. Customs are different in America, Mistress Abby. Our weapons here are kisses at two paces."

He drew her into a strong hard embrace, his head bending lower until—

Until Abigail jerked awake with a start. She sat bolt upright in bed, blinking, taking a deep gulp of air. Tumbling her hair out of her eyes, she gazed around the familiar trappings of her morning-lit bedchamber, searching for any sign of the mist, the dueling field, or Mr. Harding. It took her a moment to realize she had only been dreaming, another moment to shake off her sense of confusion. She retained the impression of Nate's mouth, hovering close to her own, warm, tempting, and she was pierced by an astonishingly sharp regret that the dream had ended.

But as she came more fully to her senses, regret fast gave way to vexation. Blast the man! Abigail thought, thumping her fist against the mattress. For the past week, Mr. Harding had been intruding upon her classroom, her solitary walks, even her teatime.

And now the cursed man was invading her dreams. She had been doing her best to ignore Mr. Harding since his disturbing declaration of war seven days ago. But that was well-nigh impossible when she seemed to bump into him every time she set foot out her bedchamber; in the hallway, in the parlor, in the garden, going up the stairs, coming down the stairs. Like her evil genius, he was always there, ever ready with some teasing remark designed to goad her into an unbecoming retort.

When she tried to teach the girls about the British monarchy or the system of ranking, he read out loud from the Declaration of Independence. When she sought to acquaint Louisa and Clarice with some lovely English ballads, he sang "Yankee Doodle" under the schoolroom window.

Abigail was now acquainted with every verse of that infernal song. The pernicious tune ran through her head each time she sat down at the pianoforte until she despaired of ever being able to play Mozart or Beethoven again.

Small wonder that she was starting to have nightmares about dueling with Mr. Harding. And wasn't it just like the aggravating man to deny her the satisfaction of shooting him even in her dreams.

With a low groan, Abigail flung off the coverlets. Glancing at the clock upon the mantel, she was dismayed to see the hour well advanced past ten. A governess was not paid to loll abed until noon. It was all the fault of sleeping in a chamber far too grand for her, and of spending half the night fretting over what devilment Mr. Harding might be brewing next.

What would it be today, she wondered wearily. More roses perhaps? Mr. Harding insisted upon dropping them outside Abigail's door, in her workbasket, pressing them between the leaves of her books. Abigail was certain he did it for no other reason than to disconcert her. He had even managed to secrete several inside her best bonnet. Abigail had not realized that until she had attempted to don the garment, and a cascade of pink petals had tangled in her hair.

That jest had nearly provoked her into complaining to Lady Harding. But what could she say—that she was being assaulted with flowers? Thus far, she had managed to respond to all of Mr. Harding's pranks with an air of superior indifference. But her forbearance was wearing thin.

As she rose from her bed, Abigail could already feel the beginnings of a headache behind her eyes. She could hear the pounding commence in her head.

Thwack! Thwack! Thwack!

Massaging her temples, Abigail frowned as she realized that the annoying thuds did not originate in her own brain but from somewhere without. A breeze fluttering the curtains told her that she had failed to close all of her windows last night. And if that was not a sure sign of how badly Mr. Harding had managed to unsettle her, nothing was.

Shrugging a dressing robe over her nightgown, Abigail padded over to the window to close it. The dull whacking sound continued intermittently. Brushing back the curtains, she peered out with mild curiosity, seeking the source of the disturbance.

She froze at the window, letting out a loud gasp. Mr. Harding stood on the lawn below, wielding a large ax. He was chopping down one of the elms lining the drive, a dying tree Abigail had heard the gardener complaining about just yesterday.

It did not surprise Abigail to see Mr. Harding turning his hand to the matter. He was forever engaged in performing some quite inappropriate task.

But what shocked Abigail beyond measure was . . . the man had stripped down to nothing but his breeches, the bared muscles of his back tightening and rippling with every blow of the ax. She had worried what distracting thing he might do next, but she had never expected him to parade half-naked beneath her window.

Common decency dictated that she close the curtains at once. But a strange surge of defiance pulsed through her veins. If Mr. Harding insisted upon displaying himself in such shameful fashion, well, then he deserved to be stared at.

Primming her mouth, Abigail remained stubbornly by the window, flinching a little at each blow Mr. Harding dealt the tree. He hefted the ax with a fluid grace, each stroke falling with an accurate, but savage energy.

No doubt he was pretending that tree trunk was her neck, Abigail thought dryly. A fine sheen of perspiration coated his skin, matting the golden hairs on his broad smooth chest. He could well have been some ancient Roman galley slave, every bulging muscle of his powerful shoulders, every taut sinew of his arms well oiled for her inspection and satisfaction.

Abigail fanned herself lightly with her hand. It was a cool, brisk morning. How strange that Mr. Harding should sweat so, or that all of a sudden she should feel so peculiarly warm.

She did not know how long she stood thus, punishing Mr. Harding with her censorious stare when she was startled by a light knock at the door.

"Come in," she called, hastily retreating from the window. She expected it to be one of the housemaids bringing up some fresh water for her washbasin.

To her dismay, Lady Harding entered the room, a tentative smile creasing her sweet, good-natured countenance.

"Good morning, my dear. I hope I do not disturb you so early?"

"Oh, n-no. I—I was just—"

Just standing at the window ogling your half-naked stepson. Abigail fought down a furious blush. Her hand crept self-consciously to the neckline of her dressing gown and then to smooth her disheveled hair. "I—I had just this minute gotten out of bed. Pray accept my sincerest apologies, your ladyship. It is not my habit to be so lazy as to—"

"Oh, tush, my dear Miss Prentiss," Lady Harding interrupted. "I told you last evening that today should be your holiday. The girls and I shall be quite occupied. We are going to pay duty calls upon some of the tenants and then take tea with the vicar's wife. I only stopped in to ask if there is any commission we might execute for you in the village."

"That is most gracious of you, your ladyship. I do have a letter to post, but I had planned to venture into Hayfield myself this afternoon."

"Then I shall place one of the carriages at your disposal."

"No, thank you, my lady. It is an easy walk, not above four miles. As the weather is fine, I shall greatly enjoy it."

"Very well, my dear."

Abigail waited for Lady Harding to take her leave. She felt quite embarrassed appearing dishabille before the mistress of the house. But Lady Harding lingered, listening intently, a tiny furrow appearing between her brows.

"What is that peculiar pounding sound?"

"Pounding?" Abigail repeated, quite aware of the continued thud of the ax in the background. She positioned herself in front of the window as guiltily as though she were hiding a man behind the curtains.

"The noise seems to be coming from outside." Her black silk rustling, Lady Harding glided across the room. She attempted to peer past Abigail's shoulder until Abigail felt obliged to step aside.

As Lady Harding looked out the window, Abigail

was dismayed to feel herself blushing. What was the matter with her this morning? She was being remarkably foolish. She had nothing to blush for. If anyone had cause to be mortified over Mr. Harding's conduct, it would surely be his poor step-mama.

Abigail expected to see Lady Harding blanch at the spectacle of her stepson swinging an ax like some half-naked savage, performing a task that should have been left to the gardener's boy or one of the stable hands.

But her ladyship only chuckled.

"Oh, Nathaniel," she said, shaking her head indulgently. "So much pent-up energy. Poor boy."

Her ladyship's smile, touched as it was with a hint of sadness, astonished and baffled Abigail. Lady Harding let the curtain fall with a deep sigh.

"At least, I am relieved to see that Nathaniel has found something to occupy his time."

Abigail heartily agreed with her ladyship. Now if only the man could be persuaded to keep his clothes on.

An awkward silence ensued, and it became clear to Abigail that Lady Harding had something else she wished to say, but was uncertain how to begin.

Delicately clearing her throat, her ladyship asked, "You—you have been content here at your new post, Miss Prentiss?"

The question caught Abigail by surprise, but she replied, "Why . . . yes. Quite content, my lady."

"My daughters have not proved too difficult to teach?"

"No, indeed. Louisa and Clarice are delightful young ladies, quick and willing to learn."

Although Lady Harding looked pleased by this praise of her daughters, she said, "I fear you must think me a most odd, neglectful sort of mother, having taught my children so little about the manners and customs of my own country. I thought it best that Louisa and Clarice be raised as other American girls were. I never expected that my daughters would have the chance of a London Season."

"I am sure they will do quite well in London, if only—" Abigail broke off uncomfortably.

"If only their older brother could be bound, gagged, and kept in a closet?" Lady Harding asked with an unexpected flash of humor.

"Just so, my lady," Abigail replied with a wry smile.

"Nathaniel can be quite charming, the best of sons and brothers. But he can also be a—a little difficult."

Difficult? Abigail arched one brow. Terming Nate Harding a little difficult was like calling Napoleon Bonaparte a trifle aggressive.

"Has Nathaniel been difficult with you, Miss Prentiss?" Lady Harding asked.

Abigail experienced a strong urge to inform her ladyship just how impossible the man had been. But Lady Harding already looked worried. No doubt Mr. Harding gave the poor woman enough anxious moments.

"No, my lady." Abigail forced her lips into a reassuring smile. "Mr. Harding has been excessively . . . spirited at times, but nothing I have been unable to handle."

"I am so relieved to hear that, my dear. I was quite concerned about you."

"About me?"

"When you are not teaching the girls, you spend

so much time closeted in your room. I feared that Nathaniel might have been teasing you."

"N-no, indeed."

"It cannot always be easy being a governess, not even a most superior one. You lead such a solitary existence." Lady Harding's eyes lit with a warm sympathy that brought a curious lump to Abigail's throat. "I simply want you to know it is not necessary in this house. I wish you could set your scruples aside enough to dine with us on occasion. I promise you, I will make Nathaniel behave himself."

It was a promise that Abigail doubted that Lady Harding could keep. But her ladyship's gentle entreaty was far harder to resist than all of Nate's more forceful demands.

"You could at least join us in the drawing room after dinner," her ladyship urged. "You would be a most welcome addition to our family circle."

The words sent a ripple of unease through Abigail. She shifted her gaze, seeking out the painfully earned wisdom of her sampler mounted on the wall. *Keep within compass!*

"Your ladyship is most gracious, but I use my evenings to prepare lessons for your daughters. I would feel quite guilty if I shirked my duties, and I really am unaccustomed to keeping late nights and—"

"It is quite all right, my dear," Lady Harding interrupted Abigail, patting her hand. "I perfectly understand."

It had been a long time since anyone had touched Abigail in such a motherly fashion. She drew back fearing that perhaps her ladyship did understand, far too much.

She felt relieved when Lady Harding finally took her leave. As soon as the bedchamber door had closed behind her ladyship, Abigail subjected herself to a severe soul-searching. Lady Harding had looked a little wistful and disappointed by Abigail's clumsy rejection of her kindness.

Was she merely being stubborn, Abigail wondered, by her continued refusals to dine with the Harding family? Yielding to Mr. Harding on any point had become as galling as a second surrender at Yorktown.

But it was far more than pride. It was principle as well, she reassured herself. Ever since that disastrous episode with Lord Eliot Windom, she had learned to take greater care. She held herself aloof from all the families she served, even above and beyond the retiring demeanor required of a governess.

It would be sheer folly to abandon her policy now. Not that Abigail feared that she stood in any danger of breaking her heart over Nate Harding. No, she was far more likely to be hanged for murdering the man.

But she could imagine herself forming an attachment to his warm and lively sisters, even the sweet Lady Harding. And it would not do, Abigail told herself sternly.

She would not be with this family that long. After the Season, she would be moving on to a new establishment. And that was the way she liked it.

Ever independent . . . always alone.

The thought sent an unexpected pang of melancholy through Abigail, and she did her best to shake it off. Likely it was only the traces of her headache making her feel so maudlin this morning or the oppressive silence of her bedchamber.

It took Abigail a moment to realize the distant thudding of the ax had stopped. She crept to her curtains to peer outside. The stubborn elm had finally been felled. Several stable hands were trussing ropes about the branches in an effort to haul them away. But there was no sign of Nate Harding. Abigail did not know whether she was more glad or disappointed. . . .

The afternoon sun dipped behind the clouds, leaving the village of Hayfield lost in shadow. But the threat of impending rain did nothing to dampen the spirits of the crowd gathered on the green outside the Cock and Bull tavern. Lusty male voices cheered on the two combatants going at it with their bare fists.

"Go to it, lad. Give him your left. Your left!"

"Have at him, sir. That's the stuff."

"Five shillings says that carrot top takes him."

"I wager a pound on the gent in the odd breeches."

Meanwhile, the gentleman in the "odd breeches" circled for an opening. The leather fringes of his doeskins slapping against his legs, Nate bared his teeth in a grimace and danced around his antagonist, a lusty redheaded farmhand with a punishing right. The burly youth topped Nate by more than a few inches and outweighed him by considerable pounds.

The farmer popped a hit past Nate's guard, his fist glancing off Nate's mouth. Nate staggered a little, but regained his balance. As Nate swiped the blood from his split lip, the redhead grinned. But his smirk faltered as Nate rushed him. He landed a series of lightning blows to the farmhand's midriff.

The redhead grunted, doubling over slightly. He took a wild swing that Nate ducked with ease. The crowd roared its approval, the wagers turning in Nate's favor. Blood rushing like fire through his veins, Nate braced himself to deliver a telling blow.

But at that moment a familiar voice rang out from the crowd, acting upon Nate like a douse of ice water.

"Mr. Harding!"

For a split second, Nate's eyes veered toward the rigid figure garbed in a gray cloak and stiff-brimmed bonnet. He never saw the meaty fist until it smacked with bone-jarring impact against his jaw.

Pain exploded in his head, and he went down hard. A collective groan of disappointment swelled from the crowd. Dazed, Nate managed to raise up onto one elbow. The world swam before his eyes, and he shook his head in a effort to clear it.

"Mr. Harding. Nate! Are you all right?"

He became aware of Abigail Prentiss hovering over him. What the devil was she doing here? She had been doing her best to avoid him for the past week. Wasn't it just like the damned woman to turn up now at such an inconvenient moment?

Beyond the blur of her gray skirts, he could see his opponent waiting for the outcome. Struggling up to a sitting position, Nate wanted to snap at Abigail to get the deuce out of the way, but he was not sure he could talk.

He tested his jaw gingerly. It hurt like hell, but it

still worked. He rose painfully to his feet, dusting off his fringed breeches.

By this time, Abigail had whipped about and was upbraiding the red-haired youth.

"How dare you, sir! Do you realize you could be fetched up before a magistrate for assaulting the lord of Ashdown Manor?"

"I landed the first blow!" Nate said. "Now do be quiet, Abby."

But it was too late. The damage had been done. Nate sensed the crowd drawing away from him with a nervous respect, and the farmhand's fists went slack, his eyes popping.

"L-lord? Surely not, miss."

"This is indeed the Honorable Nate Harding, the heir to Ashdown Manor and nephew to the present Duke of Byerly."

Nate groaned. What was the woman going to do, recite his whole bloody lineage? The youth, who had faced Nate's fists with such cocksure bravado, now quaked in his boots.

"I—I am right sorry, ma'am. Sir. I am s-sure I didn't know, not being from this village. I only d-rove in to help my grandpa fetch his chickens to market."

"Then I suggest you be about your business before you are clapped in jail—"

"That will do, Mistress Prentiss," Nate cut her off. He limped stiffly toward the boy, extending his hand. "There's naught for you to apologize for, lad. It was a good fair fight."

But the young farmer could hardly be persuaded to take Nate's hand. He was too busy bobbing awkward bows and continuing to stammer his regrets.

Nate cursed under his breath. The only real

sport he had known since he had set foot in this accursed land, and Abigail had managed to spoil it. For a few glorious moments, he had worked off some of his frustrations; had almost felt at one with this crowd of good, honest yeomen, and had been able to forget that the hands slapping him on the back, the voices urging him on were English.

They had all slunk away now, driven off by Miss Prentiss's stern governess voice, the farmers back to their stalls at the market hall, the idlers filtering back to the taproom. Nate managed to press a few coins into the redheaded goliath's hand before he, too, took to his heels.

Nate staggered over to the bench outside the tavern. He slumped down on it in a posture of disgust and defeat. Resentfully, he watched Abigail bustle about, retrieving Nate's coat from where he had discarded it in the dust.

In short order, she summoned a maid from the inn and had a basin of water and a towel fetched out. She'd have done better to have ordered him a stiff whiskey, Nate thought. Lord, what he wouldn't have given at this moment for a long cool draft of Philadelphia beer.

Abigail stripped off her gloves with an air of brisk purpose. The poke front of her bonnet shadowed her face so he could not tell what she was thinking, but he could guess.

Savage, barbaric Yankee!

No matter how he had tried to tease or provoke these past days, she had looked right through him with an air of icy disdain. Nate had a feeling if she touched him now, he would be frozen as clean through as a glacier.

"I am quite all right, *Miss Prentiss*," he said, eyeing the towel she dipped in the water with surly distaste. "I don't need you fussing over me."

"I never fuss, Mr. Harding. Now hold still." She cupped his chin as firmly as if he had been a recalcitrant schoolboy. Her fingers, far from being cold, were very warm, her touch as smooth as silk.

As she began to dab the dirt and blood from his chin, he had his first good look at her countenance. Her face was all flushed and pretty. And her eyes ... they were luminous, as soft and green as a Pennsylvania springtime. He had never thought to see the prickly Miss Prentiss looking so gentle, her brow knit with a womanly concern. He was struck by a recollection of Abigail's voice when she had first rushed to his side. Sharp with anxiety, almost frightened.

Nate. Are you all right?

Nate. She had actually called him Nate.

Well, I'll be damned, Nate thought. His mouth would have dropped open if his jaw hadn't been so sore. If only he had known that this is what it would take to thaw the lady out, he would have had his head punched in much sooner.

Her fingers continued to feather over his face, as though testing for the extent of his injuries, moving intimately over the curve of his jaw, the sensitive hollows beneath his eyes, brushing his damp hair back from his brow. Nate closed his eyes on a blissful sigh, reveling in her gentle touch, determined to make the most of this. With Abigail, who could tell just how long such a tender mood would last?

"Am I hurting you?" she asked anxiously.

"No, ma'am," he murmured.

Abigail's fingers trembled as she ran them along Nate's strong masculine jawline. She was just beginning to realize how frightened she had been when she had seen Nate squaring off with that hulking brute of a field hand. Her heart had nearly stopped when Nate had been felled by that powerful fist.

But her alarm faded to indignation as she began to suspect that Nate was not suffering as much as she had supposed, that perhaps he was enjoying her ministrations a bit too much.

"Ah," he sighed. "A touch like yours could make a man forget he ever knew what pain was."

He turned so that the hot moist curve of his lips brushed up against her fingertips. Abigail snatched her hand away at once. His eyes fluttered open, startlingly blue as ever with more than a hint of the devil in them. His slightly swollen lip, the bruise that darkened one cheek only added to the man's aura of raffish attractiveness.

"You appeared to have taken no permanent damage," she said tartly. "How fortunate that most of the blows were taken by your head."

Nate started to grin, then winced, pressing one hand to the line of his jaw. But Abigail was not about to be tricked into offering any more sympathy, a sympathy moreover that he did not deserve. Brawling in public like any common ruffian!

"I think I could manage to stand up again," he said with an unconvincing moan. "If you would just let me lean on your shoulder. . ."

But Abigail stepped out of his reach and pursed her lips. "I see nothing wrong with you, sir, except that your opponent managed to darken your daylights."

"Darken my what?"

"I beg your pardon. It is only some disreputable

slang I acquired from the brother of one of my students. It means you have a bruise forming beneath your eye."

Nate chuckled. "And what would you say I had done to the other fellow?"

"I believe you drew his cork. No, that's not right. That would mean you bloodied his nose." Abigail frowned in effort of memory, then brought herself up short. She gave Nate a reproving glance. "It is hardly appropriate for me to be teaching you boxing cant."

"No? You are clearly perishing to be teaching me something." He folded his arms across his chest, regarding her with an air of infuriating amusement. "I can read a scolding coming in those beautiful green eyes."

"It is hardly my place to scold you, Mr. Harding."

"Oh, come along, Mistress Abby. I am sure you have plenty to say to me about behavior unbecoming a gentleman and all that folderol. You might as well get it off your chest before you bust your stays."

"Mr. Harding!" But beneath her outrage, Abigail had to admit he was right. She did burn to give Mr. Harding a severe lecture regarding his infamous conduct. She struggled to contain herself a moment longer before bursting out, "Whatever could have possessed you, sir, to engage in a vulgar fistfight with that farmer?"

"You know, I don't rightly recollect, Mistress Abby. I think he may have said something unflattering about my breeches."

"You got into a fight over—over your inexpressibles?"

"It may have started out that way. I think we

eventually moved on to exchanging speculations about each other's parentage."

"This is not amusing, Mr. Harding. Have you no regard for your family, the honor of your name, to—to be disgracing yourself in this fashion?"

"Maybe no one would have known my name if you hadn't insisted upon announcing it to the entire village."

"You have no idea what English country towns are like, sir. I am sure there was a great deal of curiosity about the new lord of Ashdown Manor long before you ever arrived. You have contrived to make a wonderful first impression!"

"My impression was doing just fine until you distracted me, and got me laid out in the dirt." He levered himself to his feet, towering over her in intimidating fashion. Mr. Harding had an irritating habit of doing that, and Abigail refused to be cowed.

"The point is, sir, you did not behave like a gentleman."

"Not like an *English* gentleman, certainly," he said. "Tell me, what should I have done? Challenged that field hand to a duel and attempted to shoot his brains out?"

"One does not challenge farmers, Mr. Harding. You can only fight duels with men of your own rank and station."

"What!" He stared at her incredulously. "You mean if I am angry at some fellow, I have to check out his family background before I can fight with him? Hellfire! By that time my blood would have cooled down, and I might as well forget the whole thing."

Abigail doubted that Mr. Harding's blood ever

cooled to that extent. His eyes were already smoldering with his impatience and bafflement over English customs.

"If you dressed and acted as a gentleman should, you would not have to worry about fighting, certainly not with any rude-mannered farm laborer."

"You ought to sympathize with that young hothead, Abby. I'll bet you've wanted to darken my daylights yourself upon more than one occasion."

"I—I most certainly would never—" Abigail sputtered, but Nate touched her hand, drawing attention to the mortifying fact that her fingers were clenched into tight fists.

She forced herself to relax, expelling a deep breath. "Like most of our conversations, Mr. Harding, this one appears to be quite pointless. Seeing as how you are fully recovered, I had best be on my way."

"Do you have business in Hayfield this afternoon, ma'am, or could you simply not bear being away from me that long?"

Abigail compressed her lips, refusing to rise to his baiting. She looked about for her gloves and found them on the bench before she replied, "I came to post a letter to my sister and to view some of the sights."

"The sights?"

She could scarce blame him for the note of incredulity in his voice. Hayfield was a sleepy country village, no more than a few lanes of thatched cottages, a handful of shops, a spired church, and a modest inn. But she would have choked before admitting to Nate that her chief errand in town had been to escape the solitude of her own room.

"My guidebook assures me that the remains of a

very fine priory are located near St. Clement's Church," she said as she tugged on her gloves.

"Priory? You mean that pile of crumbling stone I passed near the graveyard?"

"That stonework dates from the fifteenth century, sir!"

"Then it's about time someone thought of putting on a new roof," he drawled.

"As a man who studied architecture, I would think you would have more appreciation for—for the sort of beauty and serenity that has withstood the buffets of time."

"I have an appreciation for beauty, at least," he said, his eyes roving over her, far too bold and warm.

Abigail's cheeks fired. The man was incorrigible. Wasting no further time, she bid him a chilly good afternoon and set off across the green. She half feared that he might attempt to follow her, but Nate clearly preferred new ale to old ruins.

He lingered by the inn as a buxom maid emerged to collect up the basin and towel from the bench. Abigail watched as the brazen girl giggled and sidled up next to Nate. He slipped her a coin in recompense for her services, and as if that were not enough, he actually bent down and kissed the hussy's cheek. The girl did not even have the decency to blush, but Abigail felt her own face growing hot.

So much for attempting to teach Mr. Nate Harding to act like a gentleman. Kissing tavern wenches in public! What next! How Abigail longed to stomp over there and take him by the ear and—

She stiffened, checking the foolish thought. Abigail did not know why she should allow Mr. Harding's outrageous behavior to vex her so. As if it should bother her one jot that the man chose to make a spectacle of himself!

She watched disdainfully as Nate slung his coat over his shoulder and followed the girl into the inn.

Good! Abigail thought with a fierce scowl. At least now that Mr. Harding was occupied elsewhere, she need not fear being troubled by him again. She could enjoy her exploration of the village in peace.

But it was a most curious thing. Neither the ruined priory, nor any of the shops, nor even the discovery of a tiny circulating library held any interest for Abigail. She found herself following the lane out of Hayfield sooner than she had intended.

It was not until she had trudged some distance that she realized she had forgotten to accomplish the one thing she had set out to do—the posting of her letter. Abigail bit her lip in vexation and thought of retracing her steps.

But the village was at least a mile back by now, and the sky had taken on a threatening gray cast. If she did not wish to be caught in a rainstorm, she had best keep moving. Jane's letter could wait another day.

It was not as though she and her sister were avid correspondents anyway, Abigail thought, as she resumed walking at a brisker rate. She was not that close to either of her siblings.

Odd that she had not minded that fact so much until she had come to stay with the Hardings. But after days of observing the playful love and warmth that existed between Nate and his sisters, Abigail had become aware that perhaps something might have been lacking in her own family.

She had no memory of her mother, who had died

shortly after Jane's birth. Her father had been a cold, self-absorbed man, and her brother was just like him. Abigail could not remember Duncan ever tweaking her curls or showing any display of fondness such as Nate did with Louisa and Clarice.

As for her sister, Jane had always been a sweet sort of wigeon, but marriage to the pompous Sir Albert Beakman had changed her greatly. Jane was now far too conscious of being Lady Beakman, a social status much superior to that of a lowly governess.

It seemed to Abigail that Jane had been waiting for years for some sign of envy on Abigail's part. She wrote Abigail glowing letters about her newest gown or carriage, the brilliant crush she had just attended at Lady So-and-so's town house. *Everyone of any importance was there and all too fatiguing, my dear.*

But Abigail had never felt the slightest jealousy of Jane's title, her pin money, her jewels, or her social connections. The times her sister came closest to inspiring Abigail with envy were those in which Jane forgot her pretensions and wrote of simple things . . . inviting an old schoolfriend in for tea or adding a new fruit tree to the garden or, more poignant still, her joy in hearing her daughter lisp her first word, *Mama*.

It was thinking of those small treasures that caused regret to gnaw at Abigail and never more so than now . . . when she trudged alone down this country lane heading back toward Ashford Manor and the Hardings, just one more family that was not hers, another house that could never be her home.

Abigail felt the prickling of tears behind her

eyes, and she blinked fiercely, quite disgusted with herself. She was allowing such depressing thoughts to overtake her more and more of late. She did not know why, but it had to stop. Having the blue devils was a luxury a well-trained governess could not afford.

Besides, while she had permitted her mind to go woolgathering, the sky had darkened. There was a decided chill in the air and the wind blew with greater insistence, scattering dried leaves in her path and tugging at the brim of her bonnet. She thought she felt the first splash of rain strike her cheek.

Huddling deeper into the folds of her gray wool cloak, Abigail quickened her pace. If she arrived back at Ashdown Manor soaked, it would be entirely due to her own folly. She was attempting to calculate how much distance she had yet to cover when she heard the pounding of hooves on the lane behind her. Glancing back, she saw a solitary horse approaching.

Abigail stepped off to the side of the road to allow the rider to gallop on past. But her heart sank as he drew close enough for her to recognize the massive roan gelding, the familiar leather-fringed breeches and broad shoulders of its master.

Mr. Harding. Abigail stifled a soft groan. Of course, it was too much to hope that the man would fail to take note of her and continue on his way. He drew the reins immediately, wheeling his horse about in a swirl of dust.

Abigail noted that the bruise beneath his eye had darkened to the same ominous hue as the sky. But his injuries did nothing to impair the ease of his slow grin as he gazed down at her, the wind lifting his ash blond hair from his collar.

"Well, Mistress Prentiss, we meet again. Don't you governesses have enough sense to get in out of the rain?"

"It is not raining yet, sir, and the house is just over the next hill." Abigail winced as she felt another drop.

"It's a good half mile down the road to Ashdown Manor yet." Sidling the horse closer, he said, "You'd best let me haul you up here on Patriot, and we'll cut through the wood."

Abigail shrank back with an icy glare, calculated to demonstrate exactly what she thought of the idea of being "hauled" anywhere.

"No, thank you, sir."

"You are going to get soaking wet."

"I will not melt."

"I daresay that granite doesn't. But you might catch your death of cold, and I've got quite an investment tied up in you. Sixty pounds." He chuckled, then his voice dropped to a coaxing note, a low purr that sent a strange warmth through Abigail. "Come along, Abby. Don't be so stubborn for once. Put your foot in the stirrup and give me your hand."

He leaned over, stretching out his own hand. He never wore gloves as other gentlemen did, leaving his palms leather-toughened, his skin bronzed.

Abigail shivered. "No! Be—be pleased to ride on, sir."

Turning on her heel, she stalked off down the lane ahead of him. But she had not gotten far when the rain broke in earnest, pelting her face and bonnet with huge drops.

She heard Nate swear and make a clicking sound to his horse. Abigail caught a dizzying movement out of the corner of her eye. Nate seemed to be urging his mount straight at her.

Before she could flee or protest, his arm lashed downward and caught her hard about the waist. He swept her off her feet, yanking her up before him in the saddle. Abigail's heart gave a frightened leap, and she had no choice but to fling her arms about Nate's neck or risk falling off.

For a moment, Abigail was too shocked to respond further, overwhelmed by a contact more intimate than she had ever known. She was crushed against Nate's chest, could actually feel the firm hard pressure of his thighs beneath her own. His arms locked tight about her in an effort to tighten his grip on the reins of his restive mount. Patriot seemed no more approving of Nate's unexpected move than Abigail was.

Her shock fast gave way to unreasoning fury. Regardless of the danger of falling, the pelting rain, the rumbles of thunder, Abigail began to struggle wildly to be free.

"Put me down at once, do you hear?" she said through clenched teeth.

"Are you insane? Hold still!" Nate urged the horse off the road, but Patriot continued to dance about, tossing his head. Abigail pressed her fists against Nate's chest and shoved, trying to loosen his grasp.

"Damn it, Abby," Nate roared. "You're going to make us both fall—"

A loud clap of thunder boomed, and Patriot bolted forward. Nate lost his purchase on the reins, and the next Abigail knew, she and Nate both seemed to be tumbling head over heels.

She landed with a jarring thud that she was certain must break every bone in her body. For several seconds she was conscious of nothing but the cold rain trickling down her neck and how much it hurt to breathe. Forcing gulps of air into her lungs, she dared to open her eyes and discovered that she laid sprawled across Nate's chest.

He stared up at her with a disgruntled expression, and she was not certain whether the flash of lightning came from across the field or was centered in his blue eyes. With a furious oath, he shoved her off him. Struggling to his feet, he shielded his eyes against the whipping rain.

Sitting up, she saw what focused his attention—the distant form of Patriot streaking for home. Nate hobbled a few steps forward but appeared at once to recognize the futility of any attempt at pursuit. The horse was halfway across the field by now.

"Hellfire!" Nate rounded on Abby, rainwater trickling down his cheeks. "Now look what you've done."

"What I've done!" She glowered up at him through bedraggled strands of wet hair. "If you had not—"

But the argument was cut short by another roll of thunder, a crack of lightning so close, Abigail thought she could feel her hair stand on end.

"Come on!" Seizing her about the wrist, Nate wrenched her to her feet. Scarce giving her enough time to gain her balance, he began yanking her across the field.

She did not know where he thought he was taking her. No place of shelter existed out here in the open, and it was the height of folly with this lightning to be heading toward the trees.

Then suddenly Abigail remembered the clearing at the edge of the woods. One of the previous owners of Ashdown Manor had constructed a folly there. Abigail had stumbled across it during one of her walks about the estate.

Gathering up her sodden skirts, Abigail ran, attempting to keep pace with Nate's longer strides. By the time they reached the folly's shelter, they were both soaked to the skin.

The folly had been constructed in the form of a small Greek temple. It was possible to escape the lash of the rain by huddling far back behind the Ionic columns. At the temple's center stood a statue of some goddess, composed and dry in her tunic, not a hair of her stone chignon out of place.

Looking at the sculpture only made Abigail more aware of her own wretched state. Her bonnet had been wrenched off during the fall and now hung about her neck by damp ribbons. Her hair tumbled about her shoulders in a heavy wet mass. Her gray cloak was doubtless ruined, permanently stained with wet grass and mud.

It was enough to make her wish to smash her fist into the goddess's smug, serene features. Instead Abigail turned on Nate. She gained a savage satisfaction from seeing him looking as miserable as herself, his hair plastered to his brow, his coat sleeve torn.

"I hope you are satisfied, Mr. Harding," she shouted above the pounding of the rain. "I could have been safely back at the house by now."

"You!" He snorted. "You don't even have as much

sense as my horse. At least Patriot had the wit to head for the stables the fastest way he could get there."

"You could have been there with him if you had only left me alone as I asked."

"Well, pardon me for attempting to come to the aide of a damsel in distress."

"I wasn't distressed until you grabbed me. In this country, Mr. Harding, gentlemen don't force their chivalry upon ladies. They don't engage in public brawls. And they most certainly don't kiss strange women in inn yards."

"What the devil's wrong with a friendly kiss? If there was ever a woman who needed the starch kissed out of her, it's you."

"I'd like to see any man ever try it!"

Nate seized her roughly by the shoulders, dragging her close. But as his head came down, Abigail managed to duck, his mouth grazing hot and angry against her cheek. She drew back her hand and dealt him a ringing slap.

His eyes glinted dangerously and for a brief moment, Abigail wondered if he was going to box her ears in return. But his hand went to his own jaw instead. Rubbing it, he glared at her and said, "It appears we may be stranded here for sometime. I've already engaged in one fistfight today. Perhaps we had better keep a healthy distance between us."

"Fine," she snapped. She flounced away from him to stand by the opposite pillar, as far away from him as she could get without stepping out into the rain. He took up his own position with his back toward her.

Like two prizefighters retreating to their corners, Abigail thought with disgust. She was not certain whether she was more upset by Nate's behavior or her own. Her loss of dignity and self-control left her feeling quite appalled.

The quiet stretched out broken only by the monotonous downpour of rain and the occasional grumble of thunder. Abigail wrapped her arms about herself and shivered, uncertain whether her chill came from being soaked to the skin or Nate's stony silence. The rain appeared likely to continue without abatement all afternoon.

Perhaps she should just make a dash for it. She could hardly end up any more miserable than she already was, and at least she could get away from Nate Harding. She had half made up her mind to go when she heard Nate approaching.

Glancing up, she saw that his brow was still knit in a look as dark as thunder. But he had stripped off his frock coat and proceeded to drape it over her shoulders.

She reached up to hand the coat right back to him. But he caught her fingers in a firm grip.

"Leave it, Abigail. Damn it, for once will you accept an act of kindness from me without trying to fling it back in my teeth?"

"Why, I—I never—" Abigail began, then stopped. It had never occurred to her that her treatment of Mr. Harding could be regarded in that light. Or that in those obstinate blue eyes she would detect something akin to hurt.

"I don't mean to seem ungrateful," she said stiffly. "But I am only the governess, Mr. Harding. I am not accustomed to anyone taking such an interest in my welfare."

"Perhaps sometimes my chivalry does get a

little—er—rough around the edges. I guess I can be as much of a bully as—as—"

"As King George during the revolution?"

"During the *war for independence*, but yes, that describes my recent behavior pretty well. This disaster is all of my making. I am sorry, Abi—Miss Prentiss."

Admitting he was wrong did not come easily to this man, Abigail could tell. Yet his gruff apology touched her more than any eloquent speech could have done.

"I am sorry, too," she said. "My own conduct was hardly above reproach. Do you realize you are the only person who has ever provoked me to such violence?"

"Felt good, didn't it?" He angled his cheek toward her. "Would you like to have a go at darkening the other eye? Then I could have a matching pair."

"No, thank you!" She felt her lips curve into a reluctant smile.

"I wouldn't blame you if you did." His teasing expression faded to one more serious. "I haven't made much of an effort to understand your English customs or anything else about this infernal country. The truth is, I have done a damned poor job of keeping the pledge I made to my father."

He swung away from her, to stare out at the rain, the storm mirrored in his remarkable eyes. "I spent most of my youth idolizing my grandfather Buckmeister, one of the most hell-raising patriots that ever lived. I learned to have a scorn for everything English. There were times when—" He winced. "I even felt ashamed of my own father, God help me.

"I understand how much pain I must have given

him, but he never once reproached me. He was a real gentleman, Abby, not like me. He possessed a quiet strength I never appreciated until—"

Nate swallowed hard. "He could have come back to England after he married Nell. Do you have any idea of why he didn't, Abigail?"

"No," she replied quietly.

"He stayed on because of me, because he knew his hotheaded Yankee son would have been miserable being dragged away from the place where he was born. So my father chose to give up his own country instead."

Nate bowed his head. "I owe him a great deal more than one year grudgingly given. Sometimes I think I owe it to my father to stay here on this land he would have loved, and that thought scares all hell out of me."

He spoke softly, but she could hear the fear, the doubt, the grief that threaded through his voice. Perhaps he did deserve some of the self-reproach he heaped upon his own head, but all Abigail could think about was comforting him.

She instinctively reached out to touch him, but stayed the gesture.

"I don't believe your father would have remained in America all those years if he had wanted such a sacrifice from you," she said. "Perhaps all he desired was for you to be more open-minded, to learn to appreciate your English heritage."

"Do you truly think it is possible for a stubborn Yankee to learn such a thing?"

"I think you could learn anything you put your mind to, Mr. Harding."

"Then teach me."

"What?"

"You're the governess. You're already teaching my sisters all this—this Englishness. Instruct me as well."

Instruct him? She and Nate Harding could scarce converse five minutes without getting into a quarrel. What would the man think of next? Abigail wondered in dismay.

"I would double your salary," he said.

"It's not a question of money." She felt a hot rush of color flood her cheeks as she stammered, "Mr. Harding, I could not possibly act as governess to a—a full-grown man."

One moreover who had grown to be such a formidable specimen of masculinity, with lips too bold, eyes too blue.

"What if I promised to behave myself?" he coaxed. "No more teasing, no flirting."

Abigail shook her head. "It would not do, Mr. Harding."

He frowned. "Very well. I admit you being my governess would be rather ridiculous."

Abigail breathed a sigh of relief.

"Then simply be my friend."

Simply? Abigail stared at him.

"I have not yet found a friend in this country," he said.

Abigail was not certain if she had ever found one. She started to back away, but he held out his hand to her, the gesture tentative, even a little shy for Nate Harding.

"Please," he said. But it was not the single quiet word that was Abigail's undoing. It was the wistfulness in his eyes, the lost look of man too far from his home.

Against her better judgment, Abigail found herself slipping her fingers into his, surrendering to the warm strength of his clasp.

It hardly surprised her when a loud crack of thunder sounded as their hands touched, like a warning, a boom loud enough to bring down the walls of Ashford Manor.

Or perhaps only the walls that Abigail Prentiss had so carefully constructed around her own heart.

Chapter 5

By mid-December, the first snowfall had arrived, blanketing the grounds of Ashdown Manor with a soft layering of white. It both amused and vexed Nate to discover that the turn in weather had not prevented Abigail from setting out upon her morning walk. Nothing deterred these sturdy English from their daily habits, but it would have been convenient just once when Nate wanted to talk to Abigail, to find her curled up cozily before the fire.

Shrugging into his greatcoat, gloves, and curly brimmed beaver, Nate set out in pursuit of her. It did not take the genius of a trail finder to be able to do so. Abby's sturdy country boots had left a clear set of footprints across the snowy lawn, and Nate soon spotted the lady herself about to forge down the path leading into the garden.

She was bundled up in her heavy gray cloak, the hood drawn over her modest poke-front bonnet. When Nate called out her name, she halted and came about looking a little surprised to see him slogging through the snow after her.

"Mr. Harding."

"Mistress Prentiss." He managed to overtake her in several long strides, rubbing his gloved hands together, his breath misting before him. "Fine morning for a walk you've chosen. Not as bad as the weather that beset poor Washington at Valley Forge, but then at least the general did not have to deal with the vagaries of one very obstinate Englishwoman. Why did you not tell me you were coming out, Abigail? I could have joined you at once and would have been spared the necessity of up-ending the house, looking for you."

The color deepened in her cheeks that were already pink with the cold.

"I am only going as far as the garden to scatter some bread crumbs for the birds, Mr. Harding. And as you can see, your sisters are not with me this morning."

"And so?" He quirked one brow. "After all this time, you still cannot be afraid I mean to pounce upon you the second we are alone? We Yankees like our creature comforts, ma'am. We never attempt to ravish women behind mulberry bushes unless the temperature is well above freezing."

A laugh escaped her as silvery as the tinkling of sleigh bells. "I did not fear anything like that, sir, but as I have often endeavored to point out to you these past months, a governess has certain proprieties to consider—"

"I thought we agreed. Sometimes you would forget about being a governess if I would forget about being a hardheaded Yankee."

"Yes, but—"

"And we are supposed to be friends now, are we not?" he reminded her softly. For a brief moment, their eyes met, their breaths mingling together in

103

the frost-struck air. Abigail was the first to look away.

"Besides, I have something important I wish to discuss with you," Nate added.

"Very well."

He offered her his arm, but she was reluctant to take it. Despite the understanding they had reached that rainy afternoon in the folly, Abigail could still be damned prickly at times. Only after hesitating, did she rest her gloved fingertips upon the sleeve of his coat. It was left to Nate to press her hand more firmly in place, to draw her snugly to his side.

As they entered the garden, the pigeons that roosted in the branches of a gnarled elm set up a cooing as though they had come to expect Abigail and her morning bounty. The neat ordering of the flower beds and walkways was lost beneath the crystalline cover of white, the only splashes of color being the bright red of the holly berries, the deep hue of the evergreens.

But Nate's gaze was drawn more to the woman at his side. He didn't know much about feminine finery, but he had grown to like the way Abigail dressed. Simple but elegant. Her modest bonnet framed her delicate aristocratic features far more charmingly than any frills would have done.

The exercise had brought a sparkle to her fine green eyes, the crisp winter air tinting her cheeks and nose a rosy pink. A few tendrils of dusky hair escaped the confines of her bonnet to curl at her temples.

Becoming aware of his lengthy regard, Abigail glanced up and raised one hand self-consciously to her face. "Why do you keep staring, Mr. Harding? Do I have a dirt smudge on my nose?"

"No, I was simply wondering how a woman who tries so hard for such a no-nonsense look always manages to appear perfectly adorable."

She frowned, withdrawing her hand from his arm at once. "Mr. Harding, that was another of our agreements. If I began joining your family for dinner each evening, there would be no more flirting."

"Sorry, Abby. Sometimes I forget."

"And," she continued severely, "you also pledged to call me Miss Prentiss when I let you coerce me into remaining in the drawing room after dinner."

"Not coerce," Nate objected. "I prefer to call it bartering."

"I call it shameless blackmail, Mr. Harding, but never mind about that. The point is I have been keeping my side of the bargain. I expect you to do the same."

Nate regarded her truculently for a moment, then expelled a long sigh. "Oh, very well. I promise to behave myself."

At least for the rest of the morning, Nate thought with a mental grin. And it could not be that far off from noon already.

Abigail turned aside from the path and produced a heel of bread from her pocket that she began to crumble and strew across the surface of the snow. Several of the pigeons fluttered down and began to peck in her wake.

As Nate watched her, he could not resist saying, "May I at least tell you, Abigail, how much your company has meant to me these past few months? You've made these autumn days pass much more pleasantly than this poor exile ever thought possible. Or is that also an unacceptable compliment?"

"No, but I believe you had some more important reason for seeking me out. Was there something in particular you wanted of me, sir?"

Was there? Nate wondered. That selfsame question had plagued him a great deal these past months. What did he want of Abigail Prentiss more than her friendship? What else could there possibly be between a very proper English lady and a rough-hewn Yankee who was still determined to set sail for Philadelphia next summer?

But to answer Abigail's more immediate query, Nate said, "I only wondered if you had seen the latest edition of the *London Post* that arrived this morning."

When she shook her head, he informed her, "It would seem that your king has finally been declared irrevocably mad."

Abigail glanced up from her flock of cooing pigeons to glance at Nate with troubled eyes. "And does that please you, Mr. Harding? I know you have been brought up to consider King George your bitterest enemy."

"I hope you know me better than that by now, Abigail. I would never rejoice in any man's misery. But I am concerned. If your king is mad, what will happen?"

Abigail dusted off the last of the bread crumbs from her gloves. "Well, a regency government with Prince George as its head has always been talked of and debated. I suppose it will have to be formed and soon."

"And how do you think that's going to affect the way England will deal with America's grievances?"

"I don't know. The prince has never sought his companions among the Whigs. If they come to power, the Whigs are noted for being a little more liberal than the Tories."

"I hope so, Abigail. In the last letter I had from my uncle, he said that our Congress is preparing to issue an ultimatum. If England does not repeal those Acts of Council, which are interfering with our shipping trade, there will be war."

Abigail tipped her head to one side, her eyes sweet and earnest. "Then I pray that Parliament does repeal the acts. I do not wish there to be war between our two countries."

"Nor do I," Nate said. There had been a time when he had been burning to teach these stiff-necked British a lesson as much as any of the war hawks back in Washington. Strange how a man's views could mellow in a few short months.

Linking Abigail's arm through his once more, Nate prepared to head back to the house. They walked together in a somber silence, but despite the threat of war, such a mood could not be maintained for long.

The sun had broken through the clouds and made the snow on the lawn sparkle, as glittering as the spangles on a lady's white ball gown. The smoke issuing from the house's many chimneys gave Ashdown Manor an air of snug prosperity, the sturdy red brick conveying an aura of timelessness, serenity.

Nate was even beginning to feel a certain grudging fondness for the estate.

"It is so peaceful here," he murmured. "It is hard to think of anything so violent as war in such surroundings."

"And yet a battle was fought once not far from here," Abigail said. "One of the minor skirmishes of our civil war. Your own ancestor took part in it, a General Sir Wyatt Harding."

Nate suppressed a smile. Her frequent lectures both amused and touched Nate. He knew she had taken great pains to study his family's history in an effort to reconcile him to his British heritage.

"Your ancestor emerged victorious that day," she continued. "He was one of the generals who fought against King Charles's forces."

"A Roundhead?" Nate pulled a face.

"You sound rather disappointed, Mr. Harding."

"Perhaps I am. By all the accounts I read in those books you gave me—"

"You have been reading the English history books I loaned you?" Abigail interrupted gleefully.

"Perhaps I did just glance through one or two of them. Enough to tell that the Cavaliers sounded like a more colorful lot than those psalm singers who opposed the king."

"An ardent Democrat like you admiring the Royalists?" Abigail's eyes danced. "You shock me, Mr. Harding."

"I shock myself a little," Nate said with a rueful grin. "But there is no getting around it. Those Roundheads were a dour bunch of spoilsports."

"Well, you can rest easy, Mr. Harding. By what I could discover, your ancestor was a dashing rebel, a Parliamentarian who sought to challenge the power of the king."

"That sounds more like it."

"So you see, Mr. Harding, you acquired your rebellious tendencies from both sides of the Atlantic."

"My *independent* tendencies," he corrected as they strolled across the lawn at an ambling pace.

"I can scarce blame you for thinking the Royalists more attractive." Abigail fetched a sigh. "When I was a young girl, I used to indulge in the most absurd fantasies about being carried off by a bold and handsome Cavalier."

Nate wondered when Abigail had stopped thinking of herself as a young girl. Too long ago, he was prepared to wager. For all the knowledge that Abigail willingly shared with him, there was one subject she rarely ever broached.

Herself.

It disturbed Nate to realize he knew little more about the lady than when she had first arrived at Ashdown Manor three months ago.

"How long have you been at this governessing business, Abigail?" he asked.

"Is this another clever way for you to determine my age, sir?"

"Oh, I already figured that out a long time ago. Now I am working on how long you have been a teacher."

After a slight hesitation, Abigail said, "I was seventeen when I took up my first position."

"Why didn't you have a Season in London, and then marry a sir somebody or other? Isn't that what your sister did?"

"Jane was always more obliging than I. She was quite willing to be auctioned off to the highest bidder. I preferred the only other option open to a lady of no fortune—becoming a governess."

"What's the matter with all the men in this country? I can't believe none of them ever had the wit to try to win you. To make you change your mind about being married."

"I had offers," Abigail replied. "As I told you, I would not wed simply for the sake of acquiring a fine house and some pin money. I would never marry any man without . . ."

"Without what?" he prompted when she hesitated.

"Without affection." She picked up her pace as though she would outstrip his persistent questions.

Nate lengthened his own stride. "And you've never once met any man you thought you could love?"

"Not that I clearly recall." It was an evasive answer. That and the way she avoided his eyes told Nate all he needed to know. So there had been some man in Abigail's past who had inspired her to softer sentiments. But what had happened to him? And who was this nameless male who could still bring that expression of melancholy to Abby's eyes?

Nate had a strong urge to badger her until she told him, an urge accompanied by a sharp stirring of— No, it could not be jealousy. That would be absurd. He was merely curious, that was all.

But it was clear that Abigail's confidences were at an end. They were nearly back at the house, and she had shrugged free of him, saying cheerfully, "I had better make haste to the schoolroom. I will have a difficult enough time settling Clarice and Louisa to any lessons today without my being late. They are in such a flutter about all the guests Lady Harding has invited for the holidays."

Nate scowled. The prospect that so excited his

sisters was one he had been doing his best to forget.

"And I suppose we won't see the backs of most of these fine ladies and gentlemen until after Christmas?" he asked.

"It is not unusual for house parties to continue as long as a month."

"A month!" Nate choked. "No one ever mentioned that."

"But these guests are all old acquaintances of your stepmother's. I am sure she would not have invited anyone you could find disagreeable."

"I have a tendency to disagree with any man who expects me to address him as 'Your Grace' or 'my lord.' " Nate heaved a long-suffering sigh. "Tell me again why I ever consented to this nonsense."

"Because you wished to please your stepmother and sisters," Abigail reminded him.

No. He had done so because he had wished to please Abigail, but it was difficult to admit such a thing, even to himself. He had never allowed any female to have such sway over him. But she had been so persuasive, insisting that inviting visitors to Ashdown Manor would be a good thing for Clarice and Louisa, give them a chance to practice their social skills. What else could Nate have done but set aside his own misgivings about playing host to a parcel of snobbish British aristocrats?

Shaking the snow from his boots, he was surprised to find Abigail regarding him gravely.

"I trust that you are not planning to do anything that—that might unnerve your guests, Mr. Harding?" she asked.

"Like seeing if any of those old cannons adorning the back lawn still work?" He grinned. "No, ma'am.

I promise to be the perfect host. If all of this helps Louisa to learn to act more like a lady, it may even be worth it."

"It is more Clarice that I have been worrying about."

"Clarice?" Nate echoed in astonishment. "Why, compared to Louisa, she's an angel."

"An angel who has been growing up this fall. You must have noticed how Clarice has blossomed, how she has turned into quite a beauty."

Clarrie? His shy, snub-nosed little sister? No, Nate hadn't noticed.

"I am concerned that Clarice may draw a deal of attention she is not prepared to handle," Abigail continued. "She is still so young. I almost wish that her emergence from the schoolroom could be delayed, that she need not make her come out in London at all this year."

"Don't fret about Clarice, Abigail. She may be younger, but she's got far more sense than Louisa. And if Clarice is to have a Season in London, it must be this spring. You know we won't be here next year."

"Of course," Abigail murmured, and she said no more. But a subdued light seemed to come into her eyes as she scraped the snow from her boots and headed into the house.

Nate followed her, wondering why he had found it necessary to remind Abigail that he and his family would be leaving England after this spring. She, better than anyone else, knew when her term of employment was scheduled to end. Perhaps the reminder has been more for himself. But how odd that it should carry with it this strong and unexpected ache.

* * *

Keeping Louisa and Clarice to their lessons proved as difficult as Abigail had feared it would be. The study of French transitive verbs held no charms compared to the elegant coach and four that lumbered up the drive about midafternoon, bearing some early arrivals.

And when word filtered upstairs that the arrivals were gentlemen, all thoughts of conjugation quite flew out of the girls' heads. Abigail dismissed her pupils, and they darted off to change their frocks for their presentation in the drawing room.

Abigail spent the rest of the afternoon busying herself with some mending. She scarce noticed when the shadows lengthened across the room or the fire began to burn low in the grate. She was much too preoccupied with her own thoughts, not altogether happy ones.

The schoolroom seemed far removed from the bustle and excitement that had enveloped the rest of the house. The visitors had likely been settled in by now, and everyone would be dressing for dinner. Abigail made no move to do so herself, doubting that her presence would be required belowstairs this evening now that there were others more important than a mere governess to fill the seats around the dining table.

A hinting of melancholy threatened to steal over her, but she fought to shake it off. Certainly she was far too old and sensible to indulge in any feelings like Ashenputel in the fairy story, being denied the chance to attend the ball.

It had been her suggestion for the Hardings to entertain houseguests, as much for their good as her own. It was past time for Abigail to slip into the background where she belonged, and remember her position as governess.

She feared she had spent far too many evenings this autumn being drawn into the family circle. It became harder each night to abandon the bright blaze of the parlor fireside and return to the dark emptiness of her bedchamber, harder still to walk away from that special warmth the entire Harding family radiated.

Abigail sighed. The schoolroom already seemed too quiet without the lively presence of the girls, without Nate's tormenting presence. Realizing how dark it had grown, Abigail moved to light some candles and then rustled over to draw closed the draperies.

The moon had risen, bright and full, spilling a silvery glow over the lawn buried beneath its deep blanket of white. What a pity it was, Abigail reflected, that the human heart could not be as easily frozen beneath a layering of ice and snow. But spring always would insist upon coming, with its warmth and sunlight, its melting thaws.

And how difficult it was, even frightening, to be faced with the threat of spring when one had spent so much time accustoming oneself to winter. Rubbing her arms, Abigail shivered.

What had she allowed to happen to herself these past few months? She had not appreciated the full impact of her own confused emotions until recently.

Nate's words spoken only that morning kept sounding through her head. *You know we won't be here next year.*

Of course, she knew that. She well recalled what

the Harding family's plans were. Why then, had Nate's reminder daunted her so?

Because during her sojourn at Ashdown Manor, she had abandoned every precept of conduct set down for a governess. She had broken her own foremost rule and become altogether too attached to the Hardings, gentle, motherly Lady Harding, the boisterous Louisa, the sweet, shy Clarice and—

And Nate?

Her folly in that quarter was probably the greatest of all. Her autumn evenings seemed to be a golden blur of moments spent challenging Nate at backgammon, debating politics with him, listening to the deep rumble of his laughter, watching him light his long ivory-carved pipe. It had disconcerted her at first, this habit of his, especially indulged in the presence of ladies. But she had grown to like the rich scent of his imported Virginia tobacco, the dreamy far-off look that would come into his eyes as he smoked and talked.

Of late, he had taken to spinning her tales of America, and she had been absorbing them like a greedy child. Nate was a born storyteller, weaving her visions of everything from his own brash Philadelphia, to the more untamed grandeur of western Pennsylvania, the wild thick forests, the majestic blue mountains, the beckoning reaches of the Ohio wilderness.

Abigail had never experienced any urge to sample the wonders of faraway places, but Nate was infecting her with such an urge.

The man had a way of making her feel warm, secure, and content.

The man had a way of making her unaccountably restless.

Abigail rested her forehead against the cooling windowpane. It was certainly better that Nate's evenings from now on would be taken up with entertaining his mother's guests. And after that, it would not be long before they all journeyed to London for the Season, giving Abigail more than enough time to start rebuilding some of the boundaries that—

Abigail's thoughts broke off as she was startled by a muffled sound coming from out in the hall. A loud, but distinctly feminine wail.

She had scarce enough time to straighten and compose herself before the schoolroom door flew open. Louisa charged into the room, her face pink with righteous indignation. Clarice trailed after her, bundled in the voluminous depths of a cashmere shawl, looking equally flushed and close to tears.

Giving Abigail no time to question, Louisa burst out, "Abby! Just wait until you see what Clarice has done."

"I haven't done anything."

"No, you've just ruined your best gown, that's all."

"No, I d-didn't. I didn't mean to. I—I was only trying to m-make it better." A rare defiance blazed in Clarice's soft gray eyes, despite the moisture dampening her thick lashes. She gave a tremendous sniff fraught with impending hysterics.

"I am sure nothing has occurred which cannot be remedied," Abigail said soothingly. Crossing over to Clarice, she coaxed the girl into parting the folds of her shawl. Abigail expected nothing worse than a stain from toilet water or too many extra bows added, which could be easily removed.

But as Clarice's shawl fell away, Abigail gave a sharp gasp. The girl had evidently been busy with her scissors, snipping away trim from her dainty sprigged muslin, lowering her décolletage to an alarming degree.

Before Abigail could recover from her shock, Nate appeared in the doorway in a state of half dress, clad in his stockings and breeches. His shirtsleeves had been shoved up as though his struggles to tie his cravat proved as great a challenge as breaking in a wild colt. The white stock hung in a disheveled state about his neck.

"What the deuce is all the commotion?" he demanded. "Is anybody hurt or—" He broke off, his eyes popping at the sight of Clarice's gown. "Hellfire!"

Clarice blushed and wrapped herself back in the shawl, her lips set in a mutinous line, half-defiance, half-shame.

"Mama will never allow you downstairs in that dress," Louisa said with a dire shake of her head.

"Mama!" Nate growled. "I'll lock you up in a tower for the next twenty-five years myself."

"You haven't got a tower," Louisa shot back.

"I'll build one. What the devil has gotten into you, Clarice?"

Under the weight of her brother's disapproval, Clarice crumpled at last. She gave a shuddering sob, her tears flowing freely.

Nate's scowl immediately vanished. "Oh, now don't start that," he said, stalking forward to pat her shoulder. "It's nothing to cry about. Just tuck some lace there or—or something."

Clarice pulled away from him. "I don't want to t-tuck lace. I am tired of always looking like an—an infant. I w-want to be elegant."

Nate stared at her, clearly astonished by these unexpected histrionics from his usually placid sister. He turned a bewildered and appealing eye toward Abigail.

"That will do, Clarice," Abigail said sternly. She produced a handkerchief. Briskly, but not unkindly, she proceeded to help Clarice dry her tears. "Of course, it is only natural you would wish to look a little more mature. But we shall have to try to find you a style that is not quite so—er—matronly."

"Matronly?" Clarice said with a doubtful sniff.

Louisa gave a choked giggle that changed to an indignant yelp when Nate administered a warning pinch.

"Yes, indeed," Abigail continued, choosing her words with care. "You don't want the sort of fashion that would only do for an *older* woman, a married lady, or a dowager or—or—"

"Or a governess," Nate put in wickedly.

Abigail chose to ignore him, knowing to her cost how easy it was to be drawn into bantering with the man. She put all her energies into soothing Clarice, convincing the girl how truly elegant a lace tucker would look with the gown, and how she knew of a hairstyle that would make Clarice appear very sophisticated indeed. She soon had Clarice restored to her customary state of calm.

"Now that you have dealt with Clarrie, pray try to do something about Nate as well," Louisa said, pulling a face at her brother's attire. "He wouldn't order a single new waistcoat made up, not even with all of our important guests coming."

"I already own as many clothes as is decent for a man to have," Nate said.

"Maybe in Pennsylvania, but not here," Louisa said. "You've got to stop tearing around with your sleeves rolled up like a Philadelphia blacksmith. And those dull brown breeches of yours are awful. I believe buff-colored or yellow ones are all the crack now."

"Miss Harding!" Abigail said in her best governess voice.

The girl glanced around, genuinely puzzled by Abigail's reproving tone until Clarice reminded her, "You know Abby doesn't like us to talk slang or discuss gentlemen's breeches."

"I wasn't discussing gentlemen's breeches. I was discussing Nate's. For all his aggravating faults, even I must admit my brother has a fine pair of legs. He ought to try to show them to better advantage."

"Louisa," Nate snapped.

Abigail was surprised to note that he appeared as discomfited as she by Louisa's remarks. A faint hint of red had crept into his cheeks.

Unperturbed, Louisa continued, "And he needs a new tailcoat of Bath superfine. So close-fitting, it reveals every flaw." She gave her brother a saucy smile. "But I have heard that a man can always pad his shoulders."

"Nate's shoulders are magnificent, as broad as an ax handle, Louisa," Clarice said indignantly. Her wide gray eyes appealed to Abigail. "You certainly don't think he would require padding, do you, Miss Abby?"

Abigail's hand fluttered to her linen collar, feeling as though it had suddenly grown too tight. It only made matters worse that she could not keep her eyes from straying in Nate's direction, the dark brown breeches that clung to his hard-muscled thighs, the white shirtsleeves pushed back to reveal the power of his forearms. And as to the breadth of his shoulders . . . No, Nate Harding had no need of padding. Anywhere.

Nate placed his hands upon his hips, but there was a certain self-consciousness in his pose far different from his usual cocksure attitude.

"Maybe I'm not what you English consider a buck of the first stare," he said. "Does the manner of my dress displease you, Abigail?"

"No! That—that is, it is not really my place to—I—I mean, of course not."

"Well what about Nate's hair then?" the incorrigible Louisa prodded. "Even if he refuses to buy any new clothes, he should at least have his hair cut, don't you think?"

Cut his hair? Oh, no. The dismayed outcry almost escaped Abigail before she could stop it. She stared at those shaggy lengths of ash blond, candle shine picking out the gold in the strands where that unruly mane rested against his collar, a blend of light and shadow. She wondered what it felt like to run one's fingers through those thick waves of silk. . . .

She wondered what in heaven was coming over her. Abigail turned briskly away, saying, "I—I am not much of an expert on gentlemen's fashions and neither are you, Louisa. And now, young ladies, I think you had better go finish dressing."

"But, Abby," Clarice started to protest, "I need you to help me mend my gown."

"Change into something else," Nate ordered. "Louisa will aid you."

Louisa pouted. "But I need Abby myself. I can't find my pearl-beaded reticule."

"We have maidservants in this house. You girls cannot expect Abigail to do everything for you. She needs to be getting ready for dinner herself."

With some firmness and a great deal of cheerful ruthlessness, Nate chased both his sisters out of the room. Then he turned back almost immediately. Tugging at the limp ends of his cravat, he stalked over to Abigail.

"By the time I master this thing, everyone will have starved. I don't suppose that you . . ." He let his voice trail off, regarding her wistfully.

Abigail recoiled at what he was suggesting. The mere idea of such a thing, of standing so close to him, the intimacy of touching his clothing in a way that only a wife or lover would dare. . . An unsettling rush of heat surged through her.

"I know nothing of—of arranging cravats, Mr. Harding. We cannot expect Abigail to do everything, remember?" As she reminded him of his own words, Nate grimaced.

"You need a valet, Mr. Harding."

"Well, I haven't got one, Miss Prentiss."

"Then perhaps one of your male guests could assist you."

"Perhaps they could," he murmured. "But it would not be nearly as much fun as if you would have a go at it."

He offered her one of his wicked, teasing smiles, filled with the kind of warmth and complicity that only long-term friends should share.

Abigail steeled herself not to respond. She had

been sharing too many such smiles with Nate Harding.

"You'd best make haste, sir, or the dinner will be quite cold before you finish attiring yourself."

"And what about you?" he retorted. "You haven't even started."

"I was not planning to come down to dinner. Now that some of your guests have arrived—"

"Oh, no, you don't, Abigail Prentiss," Nate interrupted, wagging an admonishing finger at her. "You're not going to encourage me to stuff my house with lordlings, then abandon me to deal with them. What if I start jumbling up my 'sirs' with my 'lords' and 'graces'?"

"I am sure you will do just fine, if you put your mind to the task, Mr. Harding. But, please . . . you must hold me excused."

He frowned. "Why, are you ill?"

"I—I am somewhat fatigued."

"And distressed about something. You are looking remarkably Thursday-faced."

"Friday-faced, sir. If you must acquire our dreadful slang, the expression is Friday-faced."

"Friday-faced, blue devils, whatever." Reaching for one of her hands, he cradled it between the calloused strength of his own. "What is troubling you, my dear friend?"

Dear friend. The tender words coupled with the concerned light in his eyes had a strange effect upon Abigail. She felt as though constricting bands tightened about her heart.

"N-nothing. Nothing troubles me," she said, withdrawing her hand from the warm comfort of his grasp.

"Was it Louisa?" he persisted. "Did she distress you with all that teasing about my breeches?"

"No." Abigail managed a weak half smile. "I have grown lamentably accustomed to discussing gentlemen's breeches in this household."

"Then is it something I have said or done? I know I have been damn—blasted churlish about these houseguests. But I admit the first two who have arrived seem tolerable. I may learn to enjoy this whole affair, even the Christmas ball Nell plans to give, especially if you would agree to stand up with me."

"That is quite impossible, sir."

"Why is it? You wouldn't dance with me the time we bundled the girls off to that assembly in town either."

Abigail stalked away, facing the sheltering darkness outside the windowpanes before answering in a taut voice. "You have already succeeded in coaxing me to do enough things that a governess shouldn't. I cannot allow you to corrupt me entirely."

To her dismay he followed her, standing so close behind, his voice seemed to rumble low and warm in her ear. "Ah, now I understand. You have fallen into one of those moods."

"I'm sure I don't know what you mean."

"The mood that attacks you every now and then, the urge to lock yourself in your room and dust off that little sampler of yours. *Keep within compass.*"

Abigail started at his perception. "How—how did you know about—about—"

"About your bit of stitchery? I noticed it the time I hid the rose petals in your bonnet. A fine neat bit

123

of work, though I can't say as I much favor the sentiment."

"The sampler has grown a little faded," she said. "I daresay I should stitch it over again."

"And I think you should burn the one you already have." He leaned up against the window so that she could not help but look at him, his rugged features stilled into a gentle expression. A gentleness that brought a lump to her throat.

"Has it been so great a crime, Abigail?" he asked. "Straying from your notions of 'compass' enough to enjoy yourself a little, to share a few pleasant moments with me . . . and my family?"

She swallowed. "I'm beginning to fear that it is. If not a crime, at least very wrong and very foolish. I cannot even excuse myself by saying I have always been usefully employed, giving your sisters extra instruction. Rather, I have become the pupil. Lady Harding has been very kindly helping me with my knitting and—and you have given me a new perspective on your revolution."

"Our war for independence."

Abigail gave a shaky laugh. "And oftentimes instead of teaching your sisters, I find myself sharing their confidences, listening to little secrets."

"Secrets? What secrets?" Nate demanded.

Abigail wondered what Nate would say if he knew Louisa's greatest ambition in life was to learn to drive a high-perch phaeton and have half the men in London dueling over her. He would probably be amused. But he might not be equally amused to learn that Clarice's dream was to be swept off her feet by a handsome duke like some prince in a fairy story. Abigail doubted that Nate had ever considered the possibility that one of his sisters might fall in love with and actually want to marry an Englishman.

"What have my sisters been telling you?" Nate persisted.

"Secrets are meant to be kept, Mr. Harding. That is the nature of them."

"Well, if there was ever any lady I'd trust with a secret, it would be you, Abby. You're very good at keeping them, especially your own.

"Why a lovely lady like you chooses to lead such a solitary life, I'll never understand." He crooked his fingers beneath her chin, coaxing her to look up. Abigail quivered at the warm feel of his hand against her skin, and for a moment she felt almost dizzy looking too deep into those clear lakewater eyes.

"Too often," he said, "I catch a fleeting sadness on your face I don't like to see there."

"Nonsense." Abigail eased his hand away. "I am perfectly content with my life."

"Content isn't the same as happy, and I think you know that. You don't play fair, Abigail. Our friendship is very one-sided. You know practically all there is to know about me. I just wish you trusted me enough to confide in me."

Abigail's heart pounded unsteadily. He would never know how often she had felt an unaccountable urge to confide everything to Nate, her youthful heartbreak over Lord Eliot Windom, the disappointment that seemed to have put a seal on her girlhood, how lonely and bleak she often did feel.

But she hated to acknowledge such things to herself, let alone to Nate.

"I assure you, sir, my life has been very dull,"

she said. "I have nothing of interest to confide, and you do not wish to keep your guests waiting. You'd better go."

Knowing Nate as she did, Abigail expected more of an argument, but he appeared to accept her rebuff with a good grace.

"Very well. I'll excuse you for now, from sharing secrets and from joining us for dinner. But I will expect you to come down to the drawing room later."

When she tried to protest, he silenced her by adding, "Even if you are too hard-hearted to come rescue me from the ferocious redcoats, do it for Nell. I am sure she will want your help in pouring out the coffee. You know how Louisa slops it everywhere. We can't have her scalding the breeches off her prospective dancing partners."

Abigail smiled reluctantly. When it was put that way, in terms of her being required to fill some useful function, she could not refuse.

She retired to her bedchamber to change into her best gray silk. When she judged the hour to be advanced enough, she crept downstairs. It was her intention to slip into the drawing room unnoticed and station herself behind the coffee table before the others arrived. But the hum of voices coming from the chamber told her she had delayed a little too long.

Easing open the door, she tried to enter as unobtrusively as possible, the sort of entrance to be expected from the governess. But she should have known Nate would never permit her to escape so lightly.

To her horror, he called out, "Ah, Miss Prentiss. There you are, at last."

Taking her by the arm, he propelled her to the center of the room to be presented to the guests. A portly gentleman seated by Lady Harding on the settee struggled to his feet. No one could have looked less like Nate's description of a ferocious redcoat, although the gentleman did sport crimson stripes upon his waistcoat.

"Miss Prentiss, this is Sir Harry Benton. He claims to be a cousin of Nell's, but I strongly suspect he was once one of her beaux."

Both Sir Harry and Lady Harding colored a little at Nate's teasing. Abigail managed a nervous curtsy. She did not know what the plump baronet must think of being presented to the governess of the house, but Sir Harry's manners were impeccable as he bent over Abigail's hand, saying, "Charmed, I'm sure."

There was a kindness in the man's jovial brown eyes that made Abigail suspect he would have handled an introduction to the lowest of street urchins in just the same way.

She relaxed a little until Nate called out to someone at the opposite end of the room. "Your lordship, could you please tear yourself away from my sisters long enough to come over here? I want to introduce you to our schoolmistress."

Abigail cringed as she saw the other guest was already engaged with Louisa and Clarice, admiring the chinoiserie upon the étagère.

The man's back was to her. As he slowly came around, Abigail felt as though the parlor rocked around her with enough force to shatter the figurines upon the shelf.

Her heart pounded madly as she stared at familiar waves of dark brown hair, at smooth, classically handsome features, at a smile that was still a little awkward and uncertain.

And suddenly she was equally awkward and uncertain.

Suddenly she was seventeen again.

"Eliot," she breathed.

Chapter 6

Abigail sank into a low curtsy and extended her hand toward Lord Windom. Her heart hammered in her chest, but she noted with a curious detachment that her fingers were remarkably steady for someone being introduced to the man who had once broken her heart.

Lord Windom had gone pale, but his serious gray eyes held no trace of surprise. It was almost as though their meeting was not entirely unexpected to him.

"Miss Prentiss." He took her hand within his white-gloved fingers. "How do you do? It's so good to—to—" He broke off, staring deep into her eyes. "So very good," he murmured.

Abigail could not seem to find her tongue to reply. She lowered her lashes, as absurdly shy as any debutante at her first ball.

"Ahem!" The sound of Nate clearing his throat startled both Abigail and his lordship.

"Perhaps, Miss Prentiss, you would now be good enough to help my mother by pouring out the coffee," Nate said with a taut smile. "That is, if his lordship could be persuaded to release your hand."

Abigail glanced down, becoming aware that Windom still cradled her fingers within his own. He appeared to realize it at the same time, letting go of her as though she were a hot brick.

"Oh. Certainly," he stammered, his face firing red. He retreated back to the company of Louisa and Clarice, and Abigail was only too happy to flee toward the shelter of the coffee table.

She only wanted a few moments to compose herself, to recover from the shock of seeing Windom again, but Nate followed hard upon her heels.

He drew out a chair for her, but he was frowning. As she sank gratefully onto the cushion, he leaned over and muttered, "So. You are already well acquainted with this lordship?"

"N-no, that is . . . I—I—"

"No? You just happened to guess his name was Eliot?"

Abigail blushed at the memory of her indiscreet outburst. She was relieved that only Nate had been close enough to have heard. At least, she thought she was relieved. Glancing up into Nate's face, she was not so sure.

His thick dark brows arched upward like twin thunderheads. "I could believe your guessing his name if it was Tom or Jack. But *Eliot*?"

"Of course, I know his name," Abigail said, rearranging the spoons upon the coffee tray with a frantic energy the task did not merit. "Everyone in London does."

"Ah, so you met his lordship in London."

"No, not London. I believe Lord Windom has been something of a recluse since—since—" Abigail was stunned to realize how long it had been since that day in the duke's study when she and Lord Windom had bid each other a painful farewell. Curling her fingers around the handle of the coffee urn, she said with forced calm, "I have not seen his lordship for eleven years."

"Eleven years! He must have made one devil of an impression for you still to get flustered at the mere sight of him."

"I am not flustered."

"Then why are you getting ready to pour coffee into the sugar bowl?"

To her mortification, Abigail realized that Nate was right. She set down the urn with unseemly haste. "If I seem flustered, Mr. Harding, it is because you are hovering over me. You should go and entertain your guests."

Filling several of the cups, Abigail pressed him into service, helping to hand around the coffee. But as soon as Nate had finished the task, he was once more back at her side.

"Exactly where did you say you met this Lord Windom?" he demanded.

Abigail sighed. "I don't believe I ever did say."

"Well then?"

She poured out another coffee for Nate before replying, "Lord Windom was the son of one of my previous employers."

"Which one?"

"The Duke and Duchess of Rivington."

"That was that place you worked when you were just a chit of seventeen?"

"Yes."

"And this Lord Windom was one of your pupils?"

"Of course not. Eliot—I—I mean his lordship

was well out of the nursery, by then." A smile of remembrance curved her lips. "He was far from being a schoolboy."

"Then by now he must be middle-aged. Nearing fifty, I suppose."

"Don't be ridiculous, Mr. Harding. Lord Windom cannot be much older than you are."

Nate picked up his cup, balancing it precariously on the saucer as his brow furrowed in frowning concentration. Abigail could not guess what he was thinking, but she prayed that he would not speculate overmuch on her past relationship with Lord Windom. Once she had almost confided her long-ago heartbreak to Nate, but now with Windom present, the very notion of anyone else knowing her secret left her feeling embarrassed and uncomfortable. Abigail felt relieved when Nate's attention was claimed by his stepmother. He was forced to cross the room and join in the conversation with Lady Harding and Sir Harry.

Abigail managed to recover enough that when Lord Windom, himself, approached the table for more coffee, she was able to greet him without blushing. As she accepted his empty cup, she stole a glance up at him.

Amazing how little the years seemed to have touched him. His body bore the taut slenderness of a youthful athlete. Only a few strands of silver threaded his hair, but otherwise his neatly brushed locks were of a uniform dark brown, very unlike Nate's uneven lengths, which were a riot of silken shades, gold, amber, and ash. Eliot's skin remained smooth, white, and unblemished, so different from Nate's sun-weathered face, which seemed to bear the rugged lines of his laughter, the imprint of every sorrow, every passion he had ever known.

When she handed the refilled cup back to Lord Windom, he thanked her solemnly. Their eyes met. She was stunned to discover that same glow of admiration he had offered her when she was a girl of seventeen.

She could not help but be flattered, but did she feel anything more than that? It was a question perhaps best left unanswered. Windom stared down into the steaming hot liquid, and she knew he was wanting to say something more. Eliot had never been one to rush directly into speech.

It was a habit that had always made her uncomfortable, and still did. She found herself acting likewise shy, regarding her own folded hands.

"It—it has been a long time, Abigail," he said softly.

"Yes, it has."

"You have been well?"

"Oh yes, perfectly. And you, my lord?"

"Yes . . . perfectly."

Another span of awkward silence ensued.

"I was very surprised to see you here tonight," she said at last. "I had heard that you did not often leave Derbyshire since—since . . ."

"My marriage," he filled in flatly. "That is true. My wife was something of an invalid. She preferred the seclusion of our country estate. Unfortunately, she passed away last spring."

"Yes, I saw the notice in the *London Post*. I am very sorry, my lord."

Abigail looked for some trace of grief in his face. He acknowledged her condolences with a sad kind of smile, but then Windom's smile always had been laced with melancholy, unlike Nate's that flashed like a burst of heat lightning or—

Abigail brought herself up short. Since when had Nate Harding become her basis for comparison?

"I have heard tidings of you, too," Lord Windom said. "Wonderful tales about the great Miss Prentiss that carry even to the wilds of Derbyshire."

Abigail gave a deprecating shake of her head. "I doubt a mere governess could achieve such fame."

"Indeed you have. Lady Effington does nothing but sing your praises. She told me that she despaired of her daughter ever attaining any accomplishments. But for your tuition, the child would never have been able to charm the Earl of Heatherstoke."

"Miss Effington always possessed the charm. She merely wanted a little confidence."

"Which you gave her," Windom insisted warmly. He cleared his throat and added, "I have two daughters of my own."

"How fortunate for you."

"They are sweet girls. But I have been a deal worried about their education since their mother died."

"Indeed?"

"I have had to dismiss so many governesses. Perhaps I am too exacting. But I have never yet found a woman—er—that is, a teacher that could measure up to you."

"You flatter me, my lord."

"No, I have never forgotten with what patience and kindness you tutored my brothers and sisters."

"I was very young then, and, I fear, not that competent."

"You were as clever as you were beautiful. You still are."

Windom had always possessed the ability to deliver compliments with such simplicity, such devastating sincerity. Once again Abigail felt the color rise to her cheeks.

The next moment an empty cup was slammed down on the silver tray with almost enough force to shatter the fragile china. Abigail had not even heard Nate's approach. She and Lord Windom both jerked as though Nate had driven a knife in between them.

"Oh, sorry, didn't mean to startle anyone," Nate said. "But you were so engrossed in your conversation, a man could be left to die of thirst."

Was it her imagination or did she detect a certain edge to Nate's tone? Abigail replied, "His lordship was just telling me of his difficulties in finding a governess for his daughters."

"Mistress Prentiss is already engaged," Nate said.

"Of course," Windom said. "I—I didn't mean to imply . . . that is I was not trying to steal her away from you."

"How refreshing. What a pity your countrymen don't share your scruples about theft."

Oh no, Abigail thought. So she had not been imagining things. She knew that pugnacious set of Nate's chin, that devil's glint in his eye too well. Something had happened to bring out the Yankee in him.

She hoped that Windom would not rise to the bait, but his slender shoulders had gone a little rigid. Both he and Nate squared off, rather like two wary duelists taking each other's measure; Windom the picture of cool elegance in his perfectly tailored evening clothes and snow-white cravat; Nate presenting the image of some hard-muscled frontiersman, his broad shoulders straining against the confines of his formal tailcoat.

As for Nate's cravat, he had the look of having skirmished and lost. Staring at Windom's starched perfection, one of Nate's hands crept to his own limp knot. Staring back at Nate, Windom suddenly straightened. He almost seemed dwarfed by Nate's powerful physique. Could Eliot have possibly shrunk a little over the years? It was odd, but Abigail remembered him as having been taller.

"Theft?" Windom repeated at last. "I am sure I don't know what you mean, sir."

"I was referring to your navy's practice of snatching seamen off our American ships."

"Oh, that." The grim set of his lordship's countenance eased. "Yes, I have heard something about that regrettable business."

"Regrettable? Then you don't believe your mighty British navy has the right to rule all the seas?"

"Certainly not, sir. We must contrive to get along with other nations. I salute your American enterprise, and I pray our government will soon put a stop to this shocking interference with your rights of trade."

Nate looked momentarily nonplussed. This was clearly not the answer he had been expecting from any British lord. Abigail could not resist giving him a smile of triumph as though one of her best pupils had just performed a clever recitation.

"I have thanked your mother for her invitation, but I have not yet had a chance to thank you, sir,"

Lord Windom said. "I am after all a stranger to you both. It is more kindness than I ever looked for."

"From savage Americans? Oh, we uncouth Yankees can be hospitable enough," Nate drawled. "Especially when you British are not attempting to bivouac any of your troops on us."

A soft gasp escaped Abigail. What had gotten into Nate this evening? If she could have reached his ankle to give him a sharp kick, she would have done so.

"Our two countries are no longer at war, sir," she reminded him. With an apologetic smile, she turned to Windom. "It pleases Mr. Harding sometimes to tease us all about things that happened during the revolution."

"Our war for independence," Nate shot back promptly.

Windom gave a soft chuckle. "Surely, sir, you would have been a little young to have such a clear memory of that ancient conflict."

"Oh, not Nate," Louisa called out gaily. She had joined them at the table in time to hear the last remarks. Casting a pert glance at her brother, she said, "To hear Nate talk, you would think he had been there all along, toddling at Lexington in his napkins."

"If I had been, you can be sure that even at that tender age, I would have given a better account of myself than the redcoats."

"Nate!" Louisa huffed. "You are insulting our guest."

"Not at all, Miss Harding," Lord Windom said. "I am sure Mr. Harding's pride in the success of your revolution is quite . . . understandable. Men are always stirred by the tales of war. I myself, have little knowledge of such things."

"No?" Nate sneered. "I thought that was the fate of you younger sons of the nobility, having a rank bought for you in the army."

"Many are forced into the military. Younger sons, alas, do not always have the means to choose their own destiny." His lordship directed a sad smile toward Abigail.

She could almost guess what Windom was thinking. If he had been free to choose, how different everything might have been. Abigail would likely have been his wife, the mother of his children. The thought was curiously unsettling.

"Since we don't have earldoms or dukedoms in America," Nate continued in that goading tone of voice, "fathers tend to treat their children a bit more fairly. Property is divided equally. Our systems are a little more just than yours, don't you think, *your lordship?*"

"Certainly, sir. You are to be congratulated. And now Miss Harding, I believe you promised to play me a tune." Offering Louisa his arm, Lord Windom walked away before Nate had opportunity for further riposte.

Folding his arms across his chest, Nate watched his lordship's retreat with obvious contempt. "What a charming fellow. He agrees with everything I say. If I told him the moon was cheese, he'd probably suggest we serve some at supper."

"It is called *breeding*, Mr. Harding," Abigail said repressively.

"In Pennsylvania, we breed a little more spirit, ma'am, even in our sheep."

Abigail did not wish to attract attention by engaging in a quarrel with Nate, yet she could not let his outrageous conduct go unremarked.

"Mr. Harding," she began, "I do not like to lecture you, but—"

"Good, then don't . . . though you always do look deuced pretty when you are playing at being the stern governess."

"But," she continued firmly, "you treated Lord Windom abominably just now, and after you said you would be civil to Lady Harding's guests. You promised no cannons, remember?"

"I never said anything about bayonets though."

"That is not amusing, sir!"

"Only because you have misplaced your sense of humor, Abby." He added in a manner that was almost too casual, "Do you really admire that stiff-necked fellow so much?"

"Certainly. Anyone who knows Lord Windom must do so. He is intelligent, handsome, charming, well-bred, always courteous."

Nate lifted one brow, appearing both annoyed and a little stunned by her passionate words. Abigail was rather surprised herself, realizing that her heated defense of Lord Windom sprang from her disappointment in Nate as much as anything else. Nate had been growing so much more tolerant of England and Abigail's fellow countrymen these past months. It seemed almost like a betrayal that he should be reverting back to his original scorn.

Feeling more flustered than ever, Abigail concluded, "Lord Windom has always been my ideal of the perfect gentleman."

"Yes, I suppose he would be. Damn his eyes."

"And if you could stop playing the part of Yankee ruffian for five minutes, you might recognize his merit and take him for your example. If only you could be a little proper for once, Mr. Harding, and—"

"All right! I fully comprehend you," Nate snapped, flinging up one hand as though to silence her. "If it's proper you want, then proper you shall have, *Miss* Prentiss."

His lips compressed into a hard line, he bowed and stalked away from her. Abigail watched him nervously. One never knew what Nate might take it into his head to do if he lapsed into one of his devilish tempers.

But he was as good as his word. Though not exactly cordial, he treated Windom with a studied politeness for the rest of the evening. It was strange to observe Nate behaving so stiffly and formally, and it was stranger still to be ignored by him. He made no further effort to approach Abigail.

Of course, that was quite proper behavior for the master of the house toward the governess, especially when he was entertaining guests. It was precisely the effect that Abigail had hoped to achieve with Nate. She ought to have been quite satisfied, but instead . . .

Abigail shivered, rubbing her arms. Instead she felt strangely abandoned, like a person left alone in a room where the fire had gone out.

Two weeks. Nate had never known any span of time to creep by so slowly except for during his childhood when he had been confined to bed with the measles. By the afternoon of Christmas Eve, he felt like a fox run to ground. He hid himself away in the library for once mercifully devoid of guests seeking books to read, wanting to play at billiards or ply him with a dozen foolish questions about the savages to be found in America.

At least in long-ago Boston, the minutemen had had some warning, Nate thought wryly. Mr. Revere had had the decency to rush about proclaiming, "The British are coming." Nate never knew when he was going to be pounced upon by some jovial lord eager for a hand of piquet or some lady perishing to display her accomplishments to Nate. That Miss Islingcroft had even brought her harp.

Nate was tempted to lock the library door as he stole a few minutes to clean his long bore rifle. Scarcely an appropriate activity for Christmas Eve, the season of peace, he supposed, but it was one highly suited to his mood.

Pulling a stool up to the hearth, Nate reached for the rod and commenced his task. In honesty, he had to admit that he did not find all of Nell's acquaintances that bad. Except for a few of the chattering dowagers, many of the guests were quite agreeable.

Ramming the cleaning rod down the rifle barrel, Nate sighed. Who was he attempting to fool? There was only one of the guests he actively disliked.

Lord Eliot Windom. For days now since his lordship's arrival, Nate had been trying to find one flaw in the man. Perhaps that was what made Windom so irritating. The damned fellow seemed to be just what Abby had said—perfect.

He rode well, shot well, hunted well, was knowledgeable on over a dozen subjects. He could discuss fashion with the ladies as easily as he could talk prizefighting with the men. He was always infernally polite, even in the morning before breakfast. And despite possessing a skilled French valet,

Windom even tied his own cravats, achieving starched perfection every time.

Hard as it was to admit, the thing Nate found most aggravating about the man was the way Abigail had breathed his name that first night.

Eliot.

She had never used Nate's Christian name in that way, not even when he had begged her to do so, not even after they were supposed to be friends. Not that it really bothered him. Not that he in the least cared or was jealous.

But how hotly Abigail had defended Windom against the slightest criticism. Nate wondered if she would ever do the same for him. No, more likely Abigail would tend to join in deploring the manners of that uncouth, uncivil Yankee.

If only you would try to be a little more proper, Mr. Harding. Nate thought he would never forget her reproof or the disappointment in her eyes when she held him up to Windom and obviously found Nate wanting.

Well, he'd been trying to be more of what these English considered proper these past days, trying until Nate felt as though he would burst from the effort. The devil of it was, he wasn't sure that Abigail even noticed his efforts.

She had been too busy "keeping within compass," staying in the background, playing the role of governess to the hilt, only putting herself forward when she could be useful.

But Nate detected a certain consciousness in her manner any time Windom entered the room. And more than once Nate had surprised a look in Windom's eyes when he stared at Abigail, a look that made Nate long to—what had Abby called it?—to darken Windom's daylights.

So what had been between Abigail and this Lord Windom anyway? Nate didn't for a moment accept Abigail's explanation that his lordship had been nothing more to her than the son of a past employer.

Had he been her suitor? Had she loved him once? Did she still? Did he love her? Who could tell with these blasted British? Nate had never known any breed better at concealing their feelings than the English gentry.

If Abby and Windom had been in love, what had gone wrong? Why had they never married? And the most important question of all, why should Nate give a damn? It was none of his concern, especially since Abigail had never chosen to confide in him.

Nate rammed the rod in and out of his rifle with unnecessary force. All he knew was that he would be cursed glad when these holidays were over, and he had seen the last of—

"Haloo. Mr. Harding?"

Nate cringed at the sound of too dulcet feminine tones as the library door was inched open.

Lady Selena Islingcroft peered inside the room, the ribbons on her lace cap fluttering. "Ah, there you are, sir. The footman told me I might find you in here."

"Did he, indeed?" Nate murmured. When he found out which footman, he'd have the fellow shot at sunrise. If Lord Windom was his least favorite among the houseguests, Lady Islingcroft ran a close second.

He struggled to his feet as the scrawny dowager

rustled forward, pretending to be greatly taken aback by the sight of Nate's rifle.

"Dear me, Mr. Harding," she said. "Whatever would you be wanting to do with that nasty-looking thing?"

Lady, you wouldn't want to know, Nate thought. Forcing a smile to his lips that was more of a grimace, he replied, "Just hoping to get in a little bit of sport later in the week, ma'am."

She wagged one finger at him. "Oh, you gentlemen and your shooting. My husband is the same. Oftentimes I have said to him, 'Islingcroft, I do believe you'd rather shoot than eat.' If only Islingcroft was as knowledgeable about horses as he is about his firearms."

Nate said nothing, knowing her ladyship rarely expected a comment or gave one a chance to do so.

"Even my eldest daughter Charlotte knows her papa is a poor judge of horseflesh. A clever girl, my Charlotte. One doesn't like to brag, but one doesn't often meet a girl who is both clever and beautiful."

"No, ma'am," Nate said, managing not to roll his eyes.

"Well, Charlotte and I are both in such a flutter, because here is Islingcroft planning to purchase a coach horse from your local squire. I do wish you would give Islingcroft your opinion in the matter. I live in terror of an unsound animal pulling our carriage. Why, we might not even be able to make it back home."

"Never fear, ma'am. I'll make sure you and your Charlotte get home even if I have to hitch myself in the traces."

While her ladyship cooed over his gallantry, Nate heard a choked sound coming from the doorway. He glanced up to see Abigail on the threshold. She had her hand pressed to her lips and seemed oddly unable to speak.

Her ladyship whipped about, becoming also aware of Abigail's presence. Lady Islingcroft's benign expression immediately froze.

"Oh. Does that woman want something of you, Mr. Harding?"

"That woman's name is Miss Prentiss," Nate grated.

"Yes, your sisters' governess I recall." Her ladyship gave a thin smile. "Islingcroft and I don't employ tutors. My Charlotte obtained a more superior education at a very select young ladies' seminary."

"If Charlotte were my daughter, I daresay I would have sent her away to school, too."

Her ladyship's smile became a trifle uncertain, as though puzzling for some hidden meaning behind Nate's seemingly bland remark. After obtaining Nate's promise to help Islingcroft in his selection of a new coach horse, her ladyship swept out of the room, staring right through Abigail.

Abigail still managed a very civil curtsy, and Nate could only marvel at her equanimity. He would have been more inclined to give the old harridan's backside a swift kick.

He stood a few seconds, drinking in the mere sight of Abigail. She was looking remarkably lovely today, he thought. She had taken to doing her hair a little differently, leaving off wearing her lace cap, permitting a few dark curls to escape from her severe chignon. The ringlets caressed the rose and cream of her complexion, somehow softening the delicate angles of her aristocratic profile.

The change seemed to have come about after the

day Lord Windom had arrived, Nate thought dourly.

When Abigail opened her mouth to speak, Nate cut her off, anticipating what she was about to say.

"Don't start scolding me, Miss Prentiss, about my manner to Lady Islingcroft. I have done my best to be polite to that woman."

"Has she been plaguing you dreadfully? You must remember the poor woman has five unmarried daughters to provide for."

Nate shrugged. "I've dealt with matchmaking mothers before, even back in Philadelphia. I've done my best to hint to her ladyship she is wasting her time. I'd never wed any starched-up British female who'd make a practice of calling me 'Harding' at every opportunity."

"No, I am sure you wouldn't," Abigail said softly, her eyes downcast.

She continued silent for so long, Nate was forced to ask, "Was there something you wanted of me, Abi—Miss Prentiss?"

"Actually, I have come on an errand for Louisa."

"Oh." Nate tried not to let his disappointment show. "What does the baggage want now?"

"She desired me to ask you if she and some of the young ladies might go skating on the pond."

"Hellfire!" Nate scowled. "I already told her no. She only sent you to ask because she knows you can get round me."

"Oh no, I am sure she didn't—that—that is, I couldn't."

"Oh yes, you could, but not this time. I had a good reason for saying no. I checked the pond. I don't think it's frozen solid enough to be safe."

"Then I will tell Louisa so." Abigail turned hastily from him. She was leaving, and heaven only knew when he would be permitted a few moments of her company again.

"Miss Prentiss?"

"Yes?" She glanced back with almost an eagerness in her tone.

It made Nate wish he had something profound to say. He shuffled his feet. This was ridiculous. He was feeling as awkward as he had as a raw schoolboy the first time he had asked Miss Alberta Rose Henley if he could come calling.

"Do you think this house party thing is going well?" he inquired at last. "Are the girls enjoying themselves?"

"Oh yes. Indeed."

And am I doing all right, behaving in a way to earn your good opinion? Much as he wished to know, Nate's pride kept him from asking such a thing.

Instead he said, "Besides Lady Islingcroft, have the other guests been treating you well?"

"Yes, everyone has been most kind."

Especially Lord Windom, Nate thought, his jaw hardening. But that was another subject best left alone.

"I won't tolerate anyone being rude to you," he continued. "Until we had all these people here, seeing how some of them like Lady Islingcroft behave toward you, I guess I never truly understood how hard it is for you, being a governess." He cleared his throat, before adding gruffly, "I've made things more difficult for you myself sometimes and—and I'm sorry for it."

Her green eyes softened, becoming almost luminous. "Mr. Harding, you have driven me to distraction upon many occasions, but you have always treated me as an equal. As for the Lady Islingcrofts of this world, I have learned not to mind them. I am, after all, a most superior sort of governess."

"Sixty pounds a year's worth," he said, and was gratified to tease a smile from her.

She made once again as if to leave, and he wondered if she planned to spend another evening in her room as she had been doing since the rest of the guests had arrived. But it was Christmas Eve. He would have cheerfully browbeaten her if necessary, forced her to come down and join the festivities. That is, if he wasn't trying so damn hard to behave like a gentleman.

How would someone like Lord Windom have put the matter to her?

Expelling a deep breath, he said, "Miss Prentiss, I want you to—that is, I would like it if you put in an appearance downstairs this evening. There is to be a ball and supper."

"I know." She laughed. "Clarice and Louisa have talked of nothing else. And yes, thank you, I will be down. Lady Harding has already insisted upon it. She and your sisters have even been so kind as to present me with a new gown."

"Yes, I—" Nate began, then hastily checked himself. It would never do for Abigail to know that the gown had been his notion. That would be the surest way to make her refuse it.

Nell had already coaxed Abigail into accepting the frock and attending the ball, with obviously little persuasion. Nate wondered how much Lord Windom's presence had to do with her ready acquiescence. He tried to ignore the raw sense of hurt that sluiced through him.

"I am sure I can be very useful," Abigail said, "helping to chaperon the younger guests."

"You won't be dancing with . . . with anyone?" Nate asked.

"No, after so many years, I doubt I would even remember how. I am, after all, no longer a foolish girl of seventeen."

There was a wistfulness in her voice that seemed to tear at his heart, and it echoed inside him long after she had slipped out of the room.

He yanked at his poorly tied cravat, as though it were choking him. But it wasn't the linen he was strangling on; it was Abigail's blasted notions of propriety, and he'd had about enough of them.

He didn't care what anyone thought, not Abby, not any of these oh-so-proper aristocrats, not Lady Islingcroft, and certainly not Lord Windom.

It was Christmas Eve.

And even if the shot heard around the world had to be fired all over again—Nate steeled his jaw. Tonight, by damn, Miss Abigail Prentiss, that most superior governess, was going to dance with him.

Chapter 7

The gown had never been meant for a governess. With a high waist and short puffed sleeves, the willow green ball dress was sweetly daring, the neckline just low enough to hint at Abigail's charms. The French silk clung to her skin in a way that was as soft and seductive as one of Nate Harding's smiles.

She had not had such a dress since the long-ago ball in which she had disappointed her family by refusing to cast out lures to that wealthy merchant. It had been the last party she had ever attended as a guest.

That had been the night she had informed her brother she had no intention of marrying any man who sought to purchase her like so many pounds of grain.

"What are you expecting, Abigail?" Duncan had sneered. "Some prince on a white charger to carry you off? Such things don't happen, my dear sister. Even bold handsome knights look for a lady with some dowry. All that shining armor requires considerable upkeep."

Abigail's lips twisted a little at the memory. It had been the closest her dour brother had ever come to making a jest, however painful a one. Because, of course, Duncan had been right, and Abigail had been sensible enough to recognize that. Hence her decision to become a governess, a decision that she looked back upon with no regrets except on a few rare occasions.

Like tonight.

She stared at her reflection in the mirror, her pleasure in the gown bittersweet, each rustle, each shimmer seeming to whisper of lost girlhood, misplaced dreams. For not the first time, she experienced qualms about attending the ball this evening.

Christmas, she had found, was always one of the worst times for a governess, a time calculated to make her more aware of her nebulous position in any great household. Not precisely fitting in with the revelries of the servants belowstairs and certainly not belonging at any of the parties or dinners held in the grand hall or drawing room.

That the Hardings were warm and generous enough to include her somehow only made her sense of melancholy more acute. Abigail tried to give herself a brisk shake, wondering at the feelings that assailed her: sadness, nostalgia, and a strange discontent. Perhaps it was owing to the dress, to the odd sensation of letting her hair down again to curl against her neck in loose flowing tresses. Perhaps it was owing to Windom being in the house, a shadow of her past, a constant reminder of what might have been.

But perhaps most of all, it was due to the distance that had grown up between herself and Nate these past days. It was no longer a bit of use telling herself how right that was, that their friendship had never been a proper thing.

Since the house party had begun, he had scarce spoken to her, scarce smiled at her, scarce offered her any of that drawling Yankee wisdom that somehow seemed to put everything in its proper perspective. And as hard as it was to admit, she missed being tormented by the man.

Whatever the cause of her gloom-ridden feelings, they were highly inappropriate for Christmas Eve. Even at a ball, she was certain, there must be ways to make herself useful. And that was when Abigail Prentiss was at her best, she reflected sadly. When she was being of use.

Draping a dark shawl about her shoulders, she managed to subdue the effects of the gown. If she hurried, she could arrive belowstairs in time to help with the final preparations for the ball. Darting out of her bedchamber door, Abigail hoped to slip down the corridor without encountering any of the Hardings' guests.

She didn't. She walked dead-on into Nate instead. For a moment she caught a dizzying flash of blue eyes, felt the disturbing warmth of his hands upon her arms, even through the fabric of her shawl as he steadied her.

She retreated a step with a soft gasp. Not so much because he had startled her, but because of the way he looked. Candle shine spilled over the dark outline of his powerful shoulders, the stark angles of his face. He was attired simply in a single-breasted tailcoat, satin-striped waistcoat, and tight-fitting cream breeches, a black solitaire knotted around his throat.

No gloves, no jewels, no glittering fobs, merely a look of unvarnished masculinity. He'd made an effort to tame his unruly mane, those dark gold strands swept back into a queue tied at the nape of his neck.

Although equally startled by her sudden appearance, he recovered more quickly. "Mistress Prentiss," he said. "I was just coming to look for you. I hoped to catch you before you went downstairs."

"Why? Is something amiss? Have the preparations gone awry—"

"No, Mrs. Bridges and Nell have everything well in hand. I only wanted to see you . . . to give you this." With a courtly flourish, he produced a small sprig of white roses. "I trust you will favor me by wearing these this evening."

He was being so solemn, so formal. Abigail did not think she could endure much more of this.

"Why, Mr. Harding," she said, attempting to adopt Nate's own teasing tone. "After all the petals you assaulted me with last fall, I am astonished there could be any roses left."

"These are from the hothouse. Please . . . you will not refuse them?"

She was almost tempted to do so, anything to arouse his impatience, a spark of the fire she was used to seeing in his eyes. But how could she do so when he regarded her with an expression so sweetly earnest, almost anxious.

"Thank you," she murmured, easing one hand from beneath the folds of her shawl to accept the nosegay.

"I thought you could wear them pinned in your

hair or on your gown. You are going to permit me to see the gown, are you not?"

"Well, I—I—"

"I helped my sister to select the color. It put the little shopkeeper in the village in quite a pelter, having a great oaf of a man pawing through her bolts of silk and fripperies, as you might well imagine."

Abigail was too preoccupied imagining Nate's strong, calloused fingers caressing with such intimacy the fabric that now clung to her body. A shiver coursed through her.

"You cannot mean to hide beneath that shawl all evening," he murmured. He sought with gentle insistence to pry loose her grip on the shawl.

"After I made a fool of myself invading a dressmaker's establishment, at least you could reward me with one glimpse of the result of my efforts."

She could hardly allow him to strip away the shawl, Abigail thought. That would be far too much as though—as though he were undressing her.

She permitted the shawl to slip herself, the fabric cascading off her shoulders, coming to rest in folds at her crooked elbows. His eyes made a long slow survey, the light of approval smoldering into a heat that seemed to touch, to caress, to warm Abigail everywhere his gaze rested.

She had never been one to seek compliments, but she wished Nate would say something, do anything but stare, making it curiously hard for her to breathe.

"Well?" she quavered.

"I was right," he said. "That color is exactly the same shade as your eyes. It's a perfect fit, too, which was not at all easy when we were keeping it such a secret. I kept telling those silly women they were not allowing enough room in the bodice but—"

"Mr Harding!"

His lips curved into the familiar unrepentant grin. "Do you know I have quite missed hearing you pronounce my name in those outraged accents? This house party might have been a good thing for the girls, but—" He fetched a deep sigh. "This has been the devil of a fortnight for me, Abby. I've hated every minute of it."

Abigail was astonished to find herself in agreement with him. But when he reached out to take her hand, it was almost as if the two weeks had never been. With one touch, one smile, Nate seemed able to restore the strange bond that had been formed between them that afternoon in the folly.

"Abby, there was something else I wanted to ask you," he said.

"Yes?" Her heart skittered strangely.

But before Nate could continue, Abigail heard a footfall behind her.

"Good evening Mr. Harding. Miss Prentiss." Lord Windom's cheery voice echoing down the hall had the effect of erasing Nate's smile.

His frame immediately went as stiff as the ramrod to his grandfather's musket. Abigail snatched her hand from Nate's grasp. She had composed herself by the time Windom came up to them, all handsome perfection in his black evening clothes, a diamond stickpin winking in the white folds of his cravat.

If his lordship wondered what she was doing, lingering in the corridor with the master of the house, he was too well-bred to show it. He wished both Abigail and Nate felicitations of the season, a greeting that she noted, neither of them returned with any marked enthusiasm.

"You are looking radiant tonight, Miss Prentiss," Windom said. "How fortunate that I happened upon you. I trust it is not too late to solicit your hand for the first dance?"

Abigail heard Nate suck in his breath, and she too was a little thunderstruck. It was quite unlike Eliot to be this bold about displaying his admiration for her.

"As it so happens—" Nate began.

"I—I won't be dancing," Abigail said. "Your lordship forgets that I am not really a guest this evening."

"Indeed you are," Nate growled.

"On Christmas Eve, things need not be quite so formal," Windom said eagerly. "Lady Harding quite agrees with me. I assure you, Miss Prentiss, I would not have approached you without consulting her first."

A noise escaped Nate that sounded close to a snort.

Windom turned offended eyes in his direction. "You do not think, sir, that it was correct of me to solicit my hostess's opinion before entreating Miss Prentiss to dance?"

"I wouldn't know," Nate said. "It's been a long time since I ever felt the need to ask my mama's permission for anything."

Windom flushed pink, and Abigail made haste to intervene.

"Of course, your behavior was as always quite correct, my lord."

"Then you will honor me with the first dance?"

Abigail felt pinned somehow between Nate's

glower and Windom's look of equal determination. She scarce knew what answer she mumbled, but Windom apparently took it for consent, for he beamed and thanked her.

Now that he had secured her hand for the dance, Abigail found herself wishing his lordship would go away again. But rather it appeared to be Nate on the verge of retreat.

"There was something else you wanted of me, Mr. Harding?" she reminded him.

"Nothing that is any longer of importance," he snapped. With a curt bow, he excused himself, stalking away down the hall. Abigail watched him go, with a mixture of hurt and confusion, wondering what had happened to bring about such an abrupt change in his manner.

Surely he could not be disapproving of her consenting to stand up with Windom. Why, it was Nate who had declared many times his desire to see her dancing again. And Abigail remembered at seventeen how much she had dreamed of the honor of being partnered by Windom at a ball.

So she and Nate were both getting something they had always wanted. Why then, she wondered dismally, was Lord Windom the only one looking satisfied with the arrangement?

The crimson drawing room had shed its cold and formal aspect before an aura of enchantment and warmth that seemed to emanate from the Hardings themselves. They greeted their company with a goodwill that encompassed everyone from their household guests to the invited neighboring families to the servants dressed in their Sunday finest.

The tall night-dark windows were transformed

by the festoons of winter greenery which filled the air with a crisp clean scent, the gilded elegance of the walls softened by the glow of dozens of white candles, the Yule log blazing brightly on the hearth.

Most fairylike of all was the huge evergreen tree that had been erected in the far corner of the room, its lower branches bending under a tempting assortment of cakes, confections, and gingerbread. Its presence seemed to infect even the most solemn of the guests with feelings of childlike wonder and gaiety.

Standing at the base of the tree, Abigail forgot much of her discomfiture over the recent scene between herself and Nate in the upper hall. She stared up at the shimmering branches with a degree of wistfulness as she remembered what Louisa had said earlier about the tree.

"Just one of our own customs Nate insisted upon, Abby. A bit of home."

It was a reminder to Abigail that unlike herself, Nate had a place he called home and he intended to return there. The thought caused an unexpected lump to form in her throat.

She had few memories she had ever allowed herself to cherish, and she greatly feared tonight was destined to become one of them—the only Christmas she would ever be permitted to share with the Harding family. A memory poignant and almost unbearably painful a year from hence when she was situated in another household less inclined to merrily discard the conventions, back in her true compass as a governess, which at this moment seemed a dismal prospect.

Abigail was almost grateful when she was

snapped out of her reverie by Lady Islingcroft. The woman jostled Abigail aside to stare up at the tree with frowning disapproval.

"Whatever is this supposed to be?" she demanded.

Overhearing the question, Clarice stepped forward eagerly. " 'Tis a Christmas tree, a custom we inherited from our brother's German grandpapa."

"Oh. German." Lady Islingcroft sniffed. "I was not aware that Mr. Harding had *German* ancestry."

"Well, but so does the King of England," Clarice said. She turned wide eyes toward Abigail in innocent appeal. "Isn't that right, Abby?"

Lady Islingcroft eyed Abigail as though she suspected her of spreading sedition.

"Certainly," Abigail replied. "Nor is the custom of the Christmas tree entirely unheard of in England. I believe the Duchess of York has one at Oatlands every year."

Her ladyship did not look as though she appreciated being informed by a mere governess, but the mention of the duchess apparently gave her pause for thought. Turning to her meek spouse, she said, "Oatlands. Then perhaps it is becoming a fashion. We must have a tree next year. See to it, Islingcroft."

His lordship gave a long-suffering sigh, but his reply was lost as the orchestra struck up the first strains of the opening dance.

Lady Islingcroft's attention was claimed in fussing over her daughters. Abigail took a keen and guilty pleasure in noticing that her young ladies put the Misses Islingcroft quite into the shade. No one could match Louisa's liveliness, or Clarice's modest beauty, especially with her lace all properly tucked up.

And Lady Harding, Abigail thought with fond

pride, was easily the handsomest matron in the room. It was clear that Sir Harry thought so as he led her out to dance.

And Nate . . . Was it only her partiality for the Harding family that made Abigail imagine that he stood out from all the other gentlemen in the room? He looked a breed apart, like a wild and majestic hawk swooping down amid a nest of peacocks.

Abigail could tell she was not the only female thus affected by his appearance. All about her she heard whispered speculation as to whom he would select for his partner. She caught herself watching his progress across the room with an eagerness so keen as to be almost painful, an eagerness tempered with a strange lowering of spirits.

Nate moved forward with determined stride, bowed, and extended his hand to . . . Mrs. Bridges.

"The housekeeper!" Abigail heard Lady Islingcroft huff. "Why, I never!"

"I did once," Lord Islingcroft mumbled. "Last holidays."

"That was different," his wife snapped. "This is not a servant's ball where one might be expected to condescend to—this—this is quite shocking."

So it was and so thoroughly Nate, that Abigail had to stifle an unreasoning urge to burst into laughter. After days of Nate's efforts at rigid propriety, it was an unexpected relief to see him doing something thoroughly outrageous. She perhaps should have been surprised that the rigidly proper Mrs. Bridges could have been coaxed into such a thing, but Abigail wasn't.

She was well aware how fond the servants at Ashdown Manor had become of their unconventional Yankee master. As aware as she was of how persuasive Nate's charm could be when he chose to use it.

So engrossed was she in watching Nate, Abigail quite forgot her promise to stand up with Lord Windom. That is, until he appeared before her with a solemn smile to claim her hand. Her heart gave a flutter, more of nervousness than anything else.

It had been so long since she had danced, longer still since she had dreamed of doing so with Windom. As he led her into one of the sets forming, she tried to recapture some of the feelings she had once had. She remembered how after her youthful charges had been tucked up in bed, she had sometimes crept to the banister, peering down into the duke's great hall and observing Windom dutifully going through the paces with his parents' guests. Then how her heart had ached with the desire to be Eliot's partner.

But now as she moved through the first steps of the dance with him, the reality seemed strangely flat. She caught herself instead glancing toward Nate and Mrs. Bridges, where they danced with a liveliness that made the rest of their set seem like stiff wooden marionettes.

Apparently noticing the direction of her gaze, when the movements of the dance brought them together, Lord Windom smiled and remarked, "Mr. Harding certainly is an original. He looks about to launch a new revolution."

"A war for independence, my lord," Abigail said, bristling defensively. "Do you find his behavior in dancing with Mrs. Bridges so odd?"

"I am less concerned with his choice of partner, being far too entranced with my own." As they circled, Windom added almost diffidently, "This is the first time I have ever been able to dance with you, Abigail. I always wanted to."

Then why the devil had he never asked her? The rebellious voice in her head astonished Abigail, especially since it sounded so much like Nate's.

Abigail had frequently lectured all her pupils upon the desirability of making polite conversation while dancing. But she fell mute with Lord Windom, leaving it to him to introduce another topic.

As they went down the dance, he said, "I understand that the Hardings will return to America next June. What will you do then, Miss Prentiss?"

It was not a question that Abigail felt equal to considering, especially not tonight, but she managed to reply dully, "Look out for a new situation, I suppose."

"I would be pleased to assist you. I know of several families who will be launching their daughters soon, and might welcome your particular services."

"Actually I would prefer a house with younger children." Abigail was a little astonished by her own words, having not realized her desire until she voiced it aloud. But that was exactly what she wanted, to be settled in some place for longer than a year or two. She did not know when the need had come over her, only that it was strong, the yearning to have at least the illusion of belonging somewhere.

They were separated momentarily. When they came together again, Lord Windom cleared his throat and said, "My two daughters are still quite young. They have great need of—of a woman's guiding hand."

Abigail glanced up at him, startled. "Are you offering me a position as governess, my lord?"

"No. It is not a governess I seek."

There was no mistaking his meaning or the look on his face. It was one of those rare times when Windom allowed his heart to show in his eyes. Abigail could see plainly that his regard for her was as strong as ever.

She stumbled, losing her place in the dance.

"Perhaps such things are best spoken of at another time," Windom murmured.

Abigail nodded in numb agreement, her thoughts as tangled as her emotions. Years ago, she would have leapt with joy if he had hinted that such a thing as marriage might truly be possible, but now she only felt . . . confused.

When the dance ended, she was relieved to be able to escape from him, fluttering her fan to cool her heated cheeks.

Windom still in love with her. Windom still wanting her. Oh, it was both cruel and unfair that he should broach such a thing tonight when she was already feeling so vulnerable.

Wearing such a gown, such a dark, starry winter night was enough to wreak havoc with a woman's common sense. Abigail could not imagine what more could happen to make matters worse.

Then coming about, she found herself staring directly in Nate's relentless blue eyes.

"The next dance, I believe, is mine, Miss Prentiss." He was smiling, but his voice was like tempered steel.

Abigail's pulses commenced a mad racing. She shook her head vehemently.

"You can't already have promised it to someone else," he said.

"No, I haven't, but—"

"I don't like coming in second, but I have waited

patiently while you got your fill of Lord Popinjay. Now I expect you to stand up with me."

He reached for her hand, but Abigail shrank back. She sensed that dancing with Nate would be different from Windom. Of a sudden, she could so clearly envision the slow sensuous circling, the heated touch of Nate's palm, the exchange of glances. A sensation akin to panic fluttered inside her.

"No, Mr. Harding," she said. "I—I am not dancing this evening."

He scowled. "What the deuce do you call what you were just doing?"

"Making a mistake."

"Then make one with me."

His invitation was far more dangerous, far more frightening than Nate could possibly imagine. Abigail slipped past him. Making her way blindly through the crowd, she managed somehow to escape out the door.

Fleeing across the hall, she raced up the stairs, aware that he followed. But she found herself strangely too close to tears to turn around when he bellowed out her name.

She paused long enough to answer. "P-please, Mr. Harding. This is not a good time for one of our infamous quarrels upon the stairs. You—you would not want any of your guests to come upon us."

"The guests be damned. Abigail, I am warning you. Get back down here."

But ignoring the grim note in his voice, she rushed on. Even though she could sense him closing the distance between them, once she gained her own bedchamber she would be safe.

Or so she thought. When she bolted inside the room, Nate strong-armed the door before she could close it against him. She backed away, dismayed and not a little alarmed as Nate forced his way into the room, slamming the door behind him.

Being closeted with Nate in her bedchamber sent a shiver through her, part fear and part excitement, that caused her heart to pound harder. Only the glow from the hearth illuminated his features, bathing his face in dancing shadows. She could see his countenance was flushed with some strong suppressed emotion, his eyes dark and dangerous. If the rough untamed colonial soldiers had looked anything like Nate, Abigail wondered where her ancestors had ever found the courage to go against them.

Her throat seemed to have tightened. When she managed to squeeze out her voice, it came in a breathless gasp. "Mr. Harding, this is extremely improper. If you don't leave at once, I shall scream."

"Don't be an idiot, Abigail. I'm not going to hurt you. But I want the answers to some questions, and I'm not leaving until I have them."

Abigail looked wildly about her for some line of retreat, something solid to put between them. There was only . . . her bed.

"Why did you dance with Windom when you won't dance with me?" he demanded.

How could she explain something to him she didn't understand herself?

"I—I don't know."

"Who the devil is this Windom? What does he mean to you?"

"He was my employer's son and—"

"Don't attempt to fob me off with that old tale."

"He was also the man—that—that I once fell in love with."

"Damn it! I thought as much. And he loved you?"

"I believed so," she whispered. The tears she had managed to hold at bay teemed over, cascading down her cheek. She became aware that Nate was offering her his handkerchief, the gesture brusque yet somehow gentle. But his eyes offered her no quarter as he continued, "And so why didn't you ever marry?"

Abigail dried her eyes and sniffed. "You would not possibly understand."

"Tell me anyway."

"He was a duke's younger son, and I—I was only—"

"Only the lowly governess." Nate's lip curled in scorn.

"Yes! Such differences in station make a great difference over here, Mr. Harding. The duchess had been so kind to engage me at all, overlooking my youth and my lack of references. I think that it amused her that I went against my family's wishes by becoming a governess. She admired my spirit."

"And did she still admire your spirit when you fell in love with her son?"

"No, she never expected that. Neither did Windom nor I. We—we never meant for it to happen. For a long time we kept our feelings secret, even from each other."

"Then I suppose his lordship crept in one day to ask for Mama's permission to love you?"

"No, it was I who confessed. The duchess was furious, but the duke was more understanding. He valued my honesty and gave me excellent references, helped me to find another position. He even

166

permitted me a few moments alone to say good-bye to Eliot."

"And Windom allowed you to be sent off that way?"

"What else could he do?"

"I'll be damned if I would ever let the woman I loved just walk away from me." The ferocity in Nate's voice startled her and made her feel slightly defensive.

"I told you you wouldn't understand. Eliot was quite broken up at our last farewell. He kissed my cheek and—"

"Kissed your cheek! And that was enough to make you moon after him all these years? Hellfire, madam. I'll give you something far better to remember."

She gasped as Nate dragged her into his embrace. She splayed her hands against his chest in a feeble effort to stop him.

"Mr. Harding! No!"

His eyes blazed with a strange fierce light that both frightened her and made her knees go weak. "You called him Eliot," Nate said. "You never once used my Christian name."

Abigail struggled futilely. "Mr. Harding. Please."

"Say my name!" He gave her a brusque shake. "Damn you, Abigail, say it."

His gaze seemed to burn into hers, compelling her.

"Nathaniel," she whispered, and she knew the moment his name escaped her lips she was lost. His mouth crashed down on hers, hot and avid.

Abigail moaned low in her throat, trying to resist the dizzying fury of Nate's kiss. But she felt her hands slowly slipping farther and farther up the wall of his chest until her arms wound around his neck, until nothing separated them but the thin barrier of their clothing.

Nate crushed her against him, melding her softness to his hard unyielding frame, his lips plundering hers until whatever mad passion consumed him seemed to spread to her like a wildfire gone out of control.

She kissed him back with a shocking abandon she had never dreamed herself capable of.

"Abby, Abby." He breathed her name, covering her face with kisses both fierce and tender.

She arched her head back, allowing him access to the column of her neck, shivering at the sensation of his mouth caressing her skin. Part of her knew it was wrong, but nothing had ever felt so right.

Moaning softly, she tugged the black riband free from his queue, loosening the dark golden strands, burying her fingers in the silky texture of his hair. When he sought her lips again, she accepted his kiss eagerly, shattered by the realization that here in Nate's arms, she was finding something she had been needing for a very long time.

Dimly she was aware of falling backward, landing upon the downy softness of her coverlet and pillows, Nate tumbling with her, their hungry seeking lips never breaking contact. He bore her down against the mattress, and she ran her hands feverishly over the width of his back, reveling in his musky masculine scent, the sweet hot taste of his mouth, the muscular feel of his body sprawled beside her on the bed.

Nate . . . in her bed.

Reason slammed back into Abigail like a hard and sudden buffet to the head. The delicious desire that had been coursing through her veins checked before an onslaught of panic.

Dear God in heaven. What was she doing?

She began struggling frantically, almost clawing Nate in her efforts to break free. His strength could easily have overpowered her, but he released her at once.

As he drew back, she saw his features still flushed with passion, but his eyes mirrored her own growing confusion and horror.

"Abby . . ." He panted. "I—I am sorry."

But she waited to hear no more. Overcome with shame, she scrambled off the bed and stumbled over to huddle by the window, seeking the return of sanity in the cool, dark night beyond. For long moments, she was conscious of nothing but her own ragged breathing, her thundering heart slowing to a more normal rhythm.

Then she heard the bed creak as Nate also rose. She sensed him coming to stand behind her and shrank closer to the glass.

"Please, Nate," she rasped. "Just go away."

"Abigail." His voice was unbearably gentle. "I realize that I got a little—er—swept away. But we have done nothing wrong. When two people experience such—such strong emotion, a few kisses are of no great consequence."

"Perhaps not in Philadelphia, Mr. Harding, but—but things are very different here. We English are more civilized."

"So I've noticed. It's a marvel to me your race has survived."

Abigail bit down hard upon her lip. She was about to perish of mortification, and he was making jests. He tried to rest his hand upon her shoulder, but she struck him away.

"Mr. Harding. Will you please leave my bed-chamber?"

"Not until you listen to me. Abby, I would never do anything to hurt you."

She whipped about to face him, her eyes stinging with tears. "Then are you prepared to promise me that nothing like this will ever happen again?"

A ghost of a smile touched his lips. "I'm afraid I can't do that."

"Then I must leave here immediately."

"No, you don't understand. I think I have fallen in love with you."

"You—you think what?" she gasped, uncertain whether she was more stunned or outraged.

"Damn!" He grimaced. "I am saying this badly. I know we are very different, and that anything between us seems quite hopeless—"

"So it is!"

"But if you would just listen to me—"

"I don't want to listen to you anymore," she cried. "From the first that I met you, you have done nothing but—but make me wretched and con-fused, overset all my principles of what is proper."

"Hellfire, Abby! Could you forget about your blasted English propriety for once and—"

"No, I cannot. Not ever!" Brushing past him, she stormed toward the door. Holding it open, she struggled for her last vestige of control. "The great-est favor you can do me is to simply go away and leave me alone."

Even in the room's half-light, she saw his shoul-ders go rigid, his lips compress together in a taut white line. "Very well. If that is what you wish."

He stalked out the door, and she closed it quickly, leaning up against the heavy oak. Trembling, swiping at her tears, she tried to make some sense out of what had just happened.

There was no doing so. Nate Harding had run quite mad, and he had nearly taken her with him. Pacing off her room in agitated steps, Abigail could scarce bring herself to look at her bed, the coverlets still rumpled from when Nate had attempted to wanton her.

Or she had attempted to wanton him. She was no longer quite sure which, remembering her response to his kisses with shame and an even more powerful stirring of emotion that shocked her.

How would she ever face his mother and sisters again? How could she possibly continue to abide under the same roof as him? She could not. A hopeless situation, Nate had called it.

Well, no one knew better about hopelessness than she, Abigail thought bitterly.

Yet he said he loved you, a voice inside her whispered.

No! She quelled the wistful thought ruthlessly. He said he *thought* he loved her. He had been carried away by the same insanity as she. Perhaps he had drunk too much rack punch or—or perhaps—Abigail glanced down at the disheveled remains of her gown, half slipping off her shoulder.

Very likely it was the wretched dress. She knew she should have never worn it.

Whatever had inspired Nate's feelings, she knew his mercurial nature too well to suppose his declaration of love could be permanent. Why, had she not heard all of Louisa's laughing tales of what a shocking flirt her brother was, how he had conquered the hearts of so many American ladies from the local schoolmistress to the butcher's daughter?

Perhaps they did not regard such things in Philadelphia. But here in England, for a staid governess, matters were very different.

Tomorrow, Nate would likely come to his senses and be able to forget what happened in her bedchamber. She never could, for the greatest difference between them of all was this.

He only thought he loved her.

And she was quite certain she loved him.

Abigail sagged down on the bed, the realization that she had struggled against for so long piercing her heart with arrow-like swiftness.

She buried her face in her hands and groaned. This could not possibly be happening to her again. Nate Harding could not turn out to be another Lord Windom.

No, there was no danger of that. Despite her misery, Abigail almost smiled. Two men had never been more unlike, as unlike as her feelings toward them. Comparing the tender emotion she had always nourished for Windom to her passion for Nate was like— like comparing a gentle breeze to a gale force wind.

But when and where had it possibly happened? At what precise moment had she slipped into this folly, surrendering her heart to that hardheaded Yankee? Not that it mattered, and it was useless tormenting herself with such foolish questions.

She loved him. And once again she would be forced to leave. For although Nate was not troubled by Windom's notions of rank, duty, and fortune, Nate had other notions of his own; like returning to America, like swearing that he would never wed a starched-up English bride.

And if she found such thoughts devastating, it was quite her own fault for allowing herself to forget—

Her eyes strayed to her sampler on the wall, the words barely visible in the gloom-ridden shadows.

Keep within compass, and you shall be sure to avoid many troubles that others endure.

In a burst of anger, as sudden as it was inexplicable, Abigail dashed the sampler from the wall, hearing the wooden frame splinter. Then she cast herself across the bed, weeping in a way she had not done since a girl of seventeen.

Abigail slept but fitfully that night. She bore a vague recollection of rising from her bed long enough to don her nightgown. Sometime later Louisa had peeked in at her, anxious to know why Abigail had deserted the ball so soon. But Abigail had feigned sleep, and the puzzled girl had left her alone again.

It was sometime near dawn when Abigail gave over all efforts at sleep. She crept from her bed, lighting a candle and donning her wrapper against the chill effects of the morning air. Lying awake, being miserable would do her no good. She might as well be employed with something practical.

Like writing to her sister Jane. If Abigail meant to leave the Hardings as soon as possible, she would need some place to go until she secured a new position. The prospect of staying with Jane was not alluring. Her sister would be bound to crow.

Everyone warned you not to accept that post with those barbaric Americans.

Abigail sighed. But she was not one to put off any task because she found it disagreeable.

Crossing the room in search of her small writing desk, it was then that she noticed the small folded paper lying on the carpet just inside her door.

She did not know how it came to catch her eye or even when the missive had been slipped beneath her door. But she knew with dead certainty who it was from.

Bending down, she picked up the note and unfolded it with trembling fingers.

Nate's bold careless handwriting seemed to leap out at her.

Abigail,

I know you too well not to suppose that by now you must be flinging your belongings into a trunk. The last thing I desire is to have you driven away by my reprehensible misconduct. Helen and the girls have too great a need of you to see them through this Season business.

It so happens that urgent affairs called me away. I will already have set out by the time you read this note. I doubt that we will meet again until all of you come to London in the spring.

By then, I hope you will have found it in your heart to forgive me, and our friendship can be as it once was.

> *Y'r obedient servant,*
> *Nathaniel Lawrence Harding*

For a moment, Abigail was too stunned to take in the full import of the note. Then her first thought was she had to stop him.

Nate going away. On Christmas day. He, who had

such a warm and close relationship with his family, who had doubtless never been alone before, without connections or friends. She did not believe for a second his nonsense about urgent business.

This was only an absurdly chivalrous gesture of his to prevent her from feeling awkward and obliged to leave. She could not allow him to make such a sacrifice.

There was no way of knowing when the note had been placed under her door, but if she hurried perhaps she could still prevent his leaving. It was still dark. Surely he would not be planning to set out until first light.

Scrambling for her clothing, Abigail was startled to hear a clatter in the courtyard below. Hastening to the window as she struggled into her frock, she saw a light bobbing on the carriage drive.

The groom held aloft a lantern illuminating a cloaked figure on horseback.

Nate!

Abigail tugged frantically at the window sash, but it stuck. She struggled to force it open, then pounded upon the glass, but it was already too late.

Nate wheeled his horse about and thundered down the drive, darkness enveloping him.

He was gone, and already the house seemed too still and empty.

Despairing, Abigail leaned her head against the cool glass and watched the sun come up on the bleakest Christmas day she had ever known.

Chapter 8

Nate gave a light flick to the reins, and the spirited chestnut team pranced down St. James Street. After four months, he'd become an expert at negotiating the twisting London streets and heavy traffic, even in so difficult a carriage as a high-perch phaeton. Exploring the city had provided an outlet for his restlessness, and he had needed such a thing during the endless days of a lonely winter that had finally dissolved into spring.

During his previous stay in London when he had first arrived in England, he had looked about him only to criticize. But during the past weeks, he had found much to admire in spite of himself; the grandeur of the homes in Mayfair, the bawdy excitement of Covent Garden, the bustling atmosphere of the docks, the timeless beauty of Westminster, the Tower, St. James Palace, all symbols of a proud and stubborn nation that had endured through centuries, a race of men he was discovering were not so different from himself.

It had amazed him to learn that Englishmen cherished their rights and freedoms as jealously as he. This then was the heritage his father had hoped that he would find. But Nate acknowledged he never would have done so if a certain woman had not helped him to open his eyes. A woman he had been trying to put out of his mind these past four months . . .

Nate guided the vehicle through the gates leading into St. James Park at a spanking pace, which he was soon obliged to check; the path being thronged at this hour with other coaches, riders, and idle strollers out to enjoy the mild April weather.

Nodding to recent acquaintances, Nate tried not to scowl as he scanned the paths and stretches of park ahead. He'd been barraged by letters since December from the females in his family, telling him how much they missed him.

Missed him so much that when he was finally able to wait upon them in town, he'd found no one at home except an elderly butler who had informed him that Lady Harding and the misses had gone to take the air in St. James Park, and that Mr. Harding should find them there.

How the deuce did one find anyone in St. James Park at the fashionable hour? Craning his neck, Nate studied each pair of skirts with such eager interest, several young ladies ducked behind their parasols with a giggle and a blush.

But he had to admit it was not Louisa or Clarice or even Nell he was looking for with an intensity that quickened his pulse.

It was Abigail. Despite his best efforts, Abby had consumed most of his thoughts since leaving Ashdown Manor. He'd lain awake nights, planning what he'd say to her when he saw her next, how he would find the precise words to make everything right between them again. But these noble plans were always disrupted by memories of that final scene in her bedchamber, how soft and yielding she'd felt in his arms, the sweet hot taste of her mouth, her low moans of pleasure as his lips had explored the silky texture of her throat. There had been a moment when he had been certain of her response, that the rush of desire had been equal between them, a strong current uniting them as one.

Had Abigail felt any regrets at his departure? His memories of her were enough to keep him tossing and turning in a sheen of sweat most nights until morning.

Damn! How was he ever to frame a proper apology when he wasn't really sorry? He regretted nothing of the embrace he'd shared with her except for a wish he might have behaved with a little more finesse.

I think I might be falling in love with you.

What a stupid thing to have said to a woman. He'd never been so clumsy when whispering words of endearment to any of the lasses he wooed back home in Philadelphia.

But matters had always been different with Abigail, something more existing between them than mere dalliance. He had never been able to be less than honest with her. And the truth was until that confrontation in her bedchamber, he had not been fully aware of his feelings.

He'd always known he admired the lady, valued her friendship. And on more than one occasion, her beauty had been enough to inspire him with a healthy male lust. But he had not been prepared for the almost insane jealousy he had experienced when she had danced with Windom. Nor had he known how right kissing her would feel, passion combining in him with a longing that shook him to the core of his soul, a longing to hold her fast forever.

But it could not be. Abigail Prentiss? She was the last sort of female he had ever imagined he would fall in love with. An Englishwoman. A lady so prim she would be ashamed to feel desire for him, whose response to his kisses had been to tell him to go away and leave her alone.

Hurt as he had been, he had almost been relieved to comply, saddling his horse and getting the devil out of there, doing something he had never done in his life.

Running away ... far away from the strong and daunting emotions Abigail roused in him. The time he'd spent with her had come damn close to making him forget who he was. Nate Harding, Philadelphia Yankee. No matter how much he had come to admire his father's country, his dreams and plans still lay waiting on the other side of the Atlantic. Dreams that a proper English governess could not be expected to share, a woman whose image of the ideal man was some starched-up duke's son.

So what then was Nate to do, even if Abigail could be induced to return his affections which was doubtful? Spend the rest of his life playing lord of the manor in Buckinghamshire? Give up his own dreams, the land that he loved, to become a permanent exile as his father had before him? No, never!

Nate pulled back on the reins, abruptly bringing his team to a halt. If he had any sense at all, he would turn the phaeton around and keep right on running. But before he could put such a plan into motion, he heard someone shouting his name.

"Nate!"

The sound of Louisa's familiar accents rang out across the park. Holding up the hem of her pelisse and clutching the brim of her straw bonnet, she came tearing across the grass. All thoughts of fleeing gone, Nate turned over the reins to his tiger and vaulted down, hastening across the lawn to intercept Louisa.

Loath as he was to admit it, he'd rather missed the little baggage these past months. Oblivious to all shocked stares of those passing by, he swooped Louisa off her feet into an exuberant hug, which she returned, breathless with laughter.

"Oh, Nate. You came at last and—and I can scarce believe it. You've actually bought some new clothes. A driving cloak with two capes!"

"Aye, so I did. Mind the hat, minx." As he set her down, Nate straightened his curly-brimmed beaver in time to keep it from flying off his head.

But he had hardly recovered from Louisa's onslaught when he found himself set upon by Clarice and Nell. Clarice's hug was only a little less hearty than Louisa's, and though he truly was glad to see her, he could not resist stealing a furtive peek over the top of her head.

No Abigail.

He managed to conceal his disappointment as he greeted his stepmother. But he had no sooner planted a kiss upon Nell's cheek, than Louisa commenced to scold.

"You left us without even saying good-bye, Nate."

"And on Christmas day, too," Clarice said.

"And you've hardly written a word to us all winter." Louisa pouted.

"I told you girls in my note that I had business to attend that could not wait."

"Pooh!" Louisa said. "I think you just ran off because you could not tolerate having guests at the manor, and I call it a downright shabby thing to do."

"Louisa!" Lady Harding chided. "Whatever kept Nate away from us for so long . . . well, I'm sure he had excellent reasons."

"I explained my reasons, Nell. You know I have been concerned about our trade being disrupted by the English, and I thought I could do some good by coming to London and trying to influence some of these British politicians, and I had other urgent affairs besides that—"

"Of course, you did, my dear," Nell interrupted soothingly, but there was a knowing look in her eye that rendered Nate most uncomfortable.

His explanations at least satisfied Clarice, but Louisa was still not to be placated.

"We have been in town a fortnight, and you have not come around until now to see us. You cannot have been that busy."

"I was away in Portsmouth, checking into some new ship designs for Uncle Franklin. It is a pleasant city. We might embark from there when we sail for home."

"Sail for home?" Clarice's eyes went round.

"Oh, Nate, you have not been booking passage for us already," Louisa cried.

"We have not even been to Almack's!"

"Or to Vauxhall."

"And Lady Holland has invited us to a ball next month."

"And the Prince Regent is to give a grand fete in June."

Lady Harding intervened to calm her daughters, and Nate said irritably, "I promised we'd stay for a year, didn't I? But the time will be up in June. We must soon give some thought to going back to Philadelphia."

His words seemed to cast a pall over all of them, Louisa biting her lip and fidgeting with her parasol, Clarice looking close to tears, even Nell fetching a deep sigh. And as for himself . . .

Nate compressed his lips, eager to change the subject. "And how did you find the town house that I rented for you, Nell? Is it adequate?"

"Yes, indeed. Quite lovely. We saved the large front bedchamber for you."

"Er—well, as to that ma'am, I had not planned to give up my lodgings."

"Oh," Nell said, the single syllable rife with disappointment and understanding.

"What!" Louisa frowned. "Stay in some horrid lodgings when we have all that room in the town house? That's ridiculous!"

"You have always lived with us, Nate," Clarice said.

"Things change, my dears, whether we wish them to or not." Nell's smile waxed a trifle wistful, the expression in her eyes soft and sad. "You girls are quite grown up, and it is only natural that Nate would eventually want— Sometimes partings become a painful necessity, even for those who are very fond of each other."

For a startled moment, Nate thought she might

be referring to himself and Abigail. Then it occurred to him that Nell was talking about herself.

He had sensed gentle hints in more than one of Nell's letters this past winter.

She wants to remain in England. Perhaps the girls do, too.

A sense of betrayal slashed through him, mingled with a bleak feeling of being more alone than he ever had in his life. But if he had learned one thing from these English aristocrats, it was to be better at concealing his emotions.

With forced cheerfulness, he said, "We should hardly be discussing such gloomy prospects in the middle of the park. We will only give these English fodder for gossip about those 'lunatic' Americans, and all Miss Prentiss's teaching will have been for naught."

Encouraging the girls to stroll on ahead, Nate lagged behind, linking his arm through Nell's. It was only then that he dared broach the subject uppermost on his mind.

"Speaking of Miss Prentiss," he said, with what he hoped was a casual air, "how has she been?"

"You may ask her yourself. I believe she is still down by the pond where we left her when we rushed over to greet you."

Shading his eyes, Nate peered past a line of trees. Next to the glimmering water, he could make out a familiar gray-cloaked figure. So Abigail had been here all along, must have been aware of his arrival, yet had not stirred one foot to come to him.

What did you expect? A voice inside him jeered. *That she would run to you with open arms, inviting you to toss her down upon the grass as you did on her bed?*

Nate grimaced, partly at his own folly and partly because the image he had conjured of Abigail, all blushing eagerness for his kiss, was far too appealing.

He did not realize that he had halted, staring in the direction of Abigail's distant silhouette, until Nell gave him a nudge, her voice recalling him to the present.

"I have grown very fond of our Miss Prentiss," she said. "She has become almost like another daughter to me. I would like to see her happily settled and as something other than a governess. She is still so young. I have been telling her she ought to consider marrying."

"Oh?" Nate tried not to sound too interested. "And what does she reply to that?"

"I do not think she is completely adverse to the thought." After a pause, Helen added, "Lord Windom followed us to town, you know. He has been calling upon us quite frequently."

"The devil he has! What does he want?"

"Well, I don't believe he has been calling for the sake of my company or that of the girls."

"You allow him to call upon Abigail?"

"Why should I not? The match would be a fine thing for her. Lord Windom makes a charming suitor."

"If a woman doesn't mind being courted by a man who needs to get his mama's permission first."

"I don't think there is any question of that. Both of Lord Windom's parents are deceased. And owing to his first marriage, his lordship is now wealthy and independent. Do you not think he would make Abigail a good husband, so mature, so courteous, so considerate?"

If Nell had been deliberately trying to goad him, Nate thought, she could not have done a better job of it. Clenching his jaw, he replied, "I am fully aware that Windom is Abigail's ideal of the perfect gentleman. No one else is likely to be able to compete with that."

"Perhaps. Though I cannot help remembering what your German grandfather used to say, how so many of the colonists never thought it possible to defeat the British empire either."

"What has that got to say to anything?"

Helen smiled at him. "If you cannot figure it out, my dear Nathaniel, perhaps you have been away from your stubborn Yankee roots for too long.

"Now I had best be hurrying after the girls. They are flirting with that handsome Mr. Stanway again. If you would do me just one small favor ... step down to the pond and tell Abigail we have walked on ahead."

Pressing Nate's hand, Lady Harding rustled after her daughters, leaving him a little annoyed with her cryptic remarks. But he did as she asked, stalking toward the pond, his steps only faltering when he came within speaking distance of Abigail.

She stood alone, well away from two small boys attempting to launch makeshift wooden boats, and a noisy crowd of young people, some bold-looking ladies laughing and chattering with several red-coated officers.

Her back to Nate, Abigail tossed bread crumbs upon the waters for the majestic swans. The graceful creatures put Nate in mind of Abby herself, so elegant, so serenely aristocratic, but how they could hiss when their feathers were ruffled.

The comparison almost brought a smile to his

lips, but he quelled it. Taking a step nearer, he whipped off his hat and stood, kneading the brim.

"Miss Prentiss."

The sound of his voice brought her around like the crack of gunfire. She paled beneath the modest brim of her bonnet, several dusky curls escaping to tickle the fine structure of her cheekbones. One look into those clear green eyes, and Nate well knew why he had been so damned restless.

He had been afraid he was becoming too attached to this England. But it was not a country that had seduced him. It was a woman.

"Nathan—Mr. Harding," Abigail breathed at last, the color returning to her face in a delicate flood. She stared at him as though she scarce recognized him.

Abigail had spent most of the winter convincing herself that she was not in love with Nate, that what she thought she felt was merely some romantic delusion borne of the fact she had never been kissed by a man before.

But he was not kissing her now or even touching her. He merely stood before her, hat in hand, in a stance that was unusually humble for the cocksure Nate Harding. And still her heart yearned toward him with an ache that was nigh unbearable. Her eyes devoured his stalwart figure, at once endearingly familiar and strange.

He seemed to have acquired a new air of elegance, his cloak with its multiple capes quite dashing. Yet his face had lost none of that leathery texture of the outdoorsman, his eyes just as intensely blue and his hair—

Abigail sucked in her breath as she looked in

vain for that magnificent mane of ash-gold that had once framed his face in windswept disarray.

All the composure she had struggled for, all the greetings she had rehearsed went clean out of her head.

"You—you cut your hair," she faltered.

"What?" After four months of separation, he appeared surprised that these should be the first words out of her mouth, and he had a right to be. But Abigail felt unable to help herself.

"You cut your hair," she repeated, experiencing a strange urge to burst into tears.

Nate ran his hand back through his short-cropped strands. "Well, yes, I or rather, that is, my valet did."

"*You* engaged a valet?"

"Is that so surprising? You told me I needed one. I do take heed of some things that you say."

Such as go away.

Overcome with guilt, Abigail lowered her gaze. She still felt responsible for Nate leaving Ashdown Manor, spending the winter banished from his own home and family. She did not know how Nate had fared, but the past four months for her had been wretched indeed, enduring the castigations of her own conscience, thinking about Nate, trying not to think about him, blaming him, excusing him, denying him, missing him . . . loving him.

A painful silence ensued broken only by the flutter of the swans upon the water and Nate tapping his gloved fingers against the brim of his hat.

"So," he said at last. "How are you?"

"Fine, Abigail lied. "Who could be otherwise on such a lovely spring day?"

"I know. On the way over here, I was admiring the beds."

Beds like hers ... Nate's muscular frame bearing her down upon the mattress, his lips searing hers. Heat crept into her cheeks.

She saw Nate's face likewise stain a trifle red.

"I meant the beds of flowers."

"Of—of course. The flowers are lovely. So is the pond and the swans. They are as plump as pillows—er, that is, as white as sheets—er, that is—"

Hold your tongue, Abigail, she thought with an inward groan. She was only making the matter worse. Fanning herself with her glove, she concluded weakly, "And—and how unusually warm it is."

Tugging at the neckline of his cloak, Nate agreed with her.

After another awkward pause, she asked, "Have you been enjoying your stay in town?"

"Oh, aye," he muttered. "It's been about as amusing as being tarred and feathered."

"I beg your pardon?"

"I said I have managed to keep busy. I have met some of my father's boyhood friends, and was even elected to membership at his old club, Boodle's. And I have been taking a little exercise at Gentleman Jackson's."

Abigail stifled a smile. She might have known Nate would find his way to the famous sparring salon.

He added, "I have also been visiting the bookshops and sitting in on Parliament. I was disappointed when your Prince Regent decided to retain the Tories in power."

"I am not sure the prince had any choice. From what I hear, the Whigs have no strong leader."

"Ah, well, politics sometimes makes for strange bed partners—" Nate broke off.

They exchanged another stricken glance.

This was hopeless, Abigail thought. In his parting note, Nate had wished that she might forget what had happened on Christmas Eve, that they might be friends again. But they could not even hold a conversation for five minutes without the word "bed" cropping up, without both of them being miserably self-conscious.

Never again could they share the companionship they had once known. It was a most painful realization, but it helped Abigail to settle upon a resolution she had been turning over in her mind for some time.

"Mr. Harding. I have something important to tell you."

"What is it?"

"I—I wish to end my term of employment with your family."

He frowned. "You are engaged until June, Miss Prentiss."

"Naturally, I would not expect to be paid the full amount and—"

"Hang the money. We have a written contract."

"No, we don't."

"We shook on it. It's the same thing."

"I don't recall—" Abigail broke off with a gasp as Nate seized her hand in a strong grasp.

"There!" he said hoarsely.

His touch, his standing so close was almost too much for her. Her entire frame shivered with a confused jumble of yearning and regret. She pulled away from him.

"Abby, if you are afraid I am going to plague you anymore, you needn't be. I already told Nell I plan to keep my own lodgings in town."

"No, you must not do that. Your sisters miss you so, and I feel bad enough that—that I was the cause of—" She swallowed hard, unable to continue.

"My leaving was not your fault," he said gently. "I was just as ... well, I really did have urgent business in town."

"You did?" She shot him a doubtful glance. "And were you able to successfully conclude it?"

"No. I am finding it more urgent than ever." His gaze fastened on her mouth with an intensity that caused her heart to pound harder. "I don't want you to give up your post, Abigail."

"Why not, sir?"

"Because I ... because my sisters need you."

Abigail sorrowfully shook her head. Foolish perhaps, but that was not what she had been hoping to hear.

"Clarice and Louisa are doing just fine. There is nothing else I can teach them. They have more need of you. A stern brother can do more to frighten away disreputable suitors than a governess or a fond mama. Lord Windom has been doing his best, but—"

"Windom!" Nate had been looking almost tender until his lordship's name was mentioned. But now his brow drew together in an ominous line.

"Y-yes," Abigail faltered. "Lord Windom has been most attentive since we came to town."

"To my sisters?" Nate fixed her with a skeptical eye.

Abigail was annoyed to feel herself blush. "Indeed, you should be grateful. He has discouraged several fortune hunters who have already attempted to pay court to Louisa and Clarice."

"I guess if anyone would know about fortune hunters, it would be Windom, having been such a notable one himself."

"He never was any such thing," Abigail gasped.

"He loved you, but he didn't marry you, did he? All because he had to get himself an heiress."

"It is not the same thing at all. Windom was bound by duty, by obligations to his family, by—by . . ." Abigail trailed off into incoherency, not knowing why Nate's blunt words should fluster her so. Perhaps because they had a painful ring of truth to them.

"You should be thanking his lordship, instead of criticizing him," she said. "Eliot has even kindly promised to get your sisters vouchers for Almack's. His mother was a great friend of Lady Jersey's, you know."

Far from looking grateful, anger flashed into Nate's eyes.

"Windom can keep his damned kindnesses to himself. I am quite capable of looking out for my own family."

"We are talking about obtaining vouchers to Almack's, Mr. Harding, not hewing a home out of the wilderness."

"It so happens, Miss Prentiss, that I have spent much of my time this winter paying calls, dragging myself out to dinners, and being introduced to many influential members of your precious *ton*. It seems that if one is witty and amusing enough, defects such as being an American can be overlooked in London. I've already been given the blasted vouchers by Lady Sefton."

Abigail gaped at him, and her amazement only added fuel to Nate's rising temper.

"You all might have known I would find a way to do so," he said. "I've always done my cursed best to get my sisters what they want."

"It was difficult for us to guess anything of your intentions when you just simply leaped on your horse and vanished one night."

"You told me to go away, damn it!"

"You didn't have to take me so literally."

They stood for a moment, glaring into each other's eyes. Hellfire! Nate thought. They were quarreling again, and that was the last thing he had intended. He feared he was never going to be able to talk rationally to Abigail again, not unless he was able to kiss all blazes out of her first.

Pacing off a few steps, he raked his hand through his hair, frustration coursing through him.

"The trouble is," he said bitterly, "I didn't run far enough away from you. I should have taken the first ship back to Philadelphia where things were far less complicated, where I knew what the devil I wanted to do with the rest of my life. I was a narrow-minded, opinionated Yankee before I ever met you, Abigail Prentiss, but at least I was content."

She flinched at his words, but she drew herself up with chilling dignity. "Forgive me if I have done anything to tamper with your ignorance, Mr. Harding. You have not had the most salutary effect on me either. Now if you will excuse me, I must go.

I was supposed to meet someone this afternoon, and he has just arrived."

Nate followed the direction of her gaze, and stifled an oath at the sight of a handsome low-perch phaeton being drawn to a halt on the pathside ahead. Two little girls crowded close on the seat next to a familiar elegant male figure.

Windom, of course, and wearing a cloak with—damn him—three capes. The fellow had better timing than the blasted British when they took New York.

"His lordship desires to present me to his daughters," Abigail said, then added stiffly, "If you would care to accompany me, I am sure his lordship would be delighted to renew your acquaintance."

"No, thank you, ma'am. The delight wouldn't be mutual."

Jamming his hat back on his head, he stalked away from her, feeling as churlish as a jealous schoolboy. Though he despised himself, he could not resist the urge to pause and look back.

Nate watched Windom sweep Abigail a magnificent bow, before turning to lift his two daughters down from the carriage for her inspection. Even from a distance, Nate could tell what perfect paragons they were in their matching pink cloaks and bonnets.

Now that was low, Nate thought with a heavy scowl, using little angels with bouncing gold curls to charm Abigail.

"I could give you daughters, Abby," he murmured. "Far more spirited than those china dolls. And bold sons, too."

He was shaken by the realization he wanted to do just that, make love to her, plant his seed deep inside her, raise a family with her, grow old together. He'd often wondered how his father had been able to give up everything for his mother—his English home, his heritage, even the approval of his family.

But seeing Abigail again after such a painful separation made everything so clear. The prospect of parting from her, losing her forever was like having a hole the size of a cannon shot tear through his heart. In that moment, Nate knew he was willing to surrender anything for her, his country, his name, his very soul.

He loved her. It was as simple as that.

But as he watched Abigail slip her hand into Windom's, he feared that such understanding had come far too late.

Chapter 9

Abigail laid her wool skirt out upon the bed, preparing to pack it away in the depths of her traveling trunk. Outside the rain beat against the town house window, the ever-changeable spring weather turning what had been a sunny afternoon into a gray, dreary evening.

Abigail folded and refolded the skirt with a precision that was unnecessary. But such excessive attention to detail came far easier than glancing up at Clarice's and Louisa's woebegone faces as they lingered by the bed, watching her pack.

"I can't believe you are going away, Abby," Louisa said.

Abigail placed the skirt in the trunk with a manner of assumed briskness. She had already packed some of her favorite books. Her hand knocked up against one that Nate had given her, Thomas Jefferson's *Notes on Virginia*. Between the leaves she had pressed the white roses Nate had presented her with on Christmas Eve. The dried petals scattered throughout her clothes, and she shifted her skirt atop the flower remnants before Louisa and Clarice could notice.

"You are abandoning us in the middle of the Season!" Louisa continued to wail.

"You girls have so many new acquaintances and admirers now. You will hardly feel the loss of one old governess."

"I thought you were more than our governess," Clarice said with a tiny catch in her voice. "I thought you were our friend."

The girl's words only seemed to add to the weight Abigail felt pressing down upon her heart. Her vision blurred, but she blinked her eyes fiercely and moved toward the wardrobe to haul out more of her clothes. Her gaze fell upon the green silk gown she had worn the night of the Christmas ball. The dress seemed to shimmer with too many memories, of the dance she had not shared with Nate, of the kiss that she had.

"Have we done something wrong?" Louisa asked. "Have we been flirting too much or—or behaving too awkwardly?"

"I've tried to remember to keep my lace well tucked," Clarice added. "Have we made you ashamed of us, Abby?"

"Oh, no, my dears!" Abigail cried. Once more she had to pause to keep her emotions in check. "You have always made me feel—That is, I have never had another such two pupils that I—I—I have been very proud to have been your governess . . . and your friend."

Her back to the girls, Abigail swiped at her eyes. Keep within compass. Why, oh, why had she ever forgotten that rule? She shoved the green ball dress

196

aside, dragging out one of her serviceable gray gowns to pack instead.

"Then I'll bet it's something Nate did at the park today," Louisa said. "That blasted brother of mine and his miserable temper." Her indignation quickly faded to a more coaxing note. "But if he said anything to offend you, Abby, he didn't mean it. You *know* how he is. One minute he's tweaking your curls and tormenting you enough to want to murder him, and the next he's presenting you with tickets to Almack's. He can be so exasperating and obstinate and—and then completely wonderful."

Abigail didn't need Louisa to tell her that. She perfectly understood the vagaries of Nate's character. He was the sort of man who would tease you for being so silly as to walk out in the rain, but he would keep a few paces ahead, laying down his cloak so you didn't get your feet wet.

"My going away has absolutely nothing to do with your brother, Louisa," Abigail said, although she nearly choked on the lie. "It is only that I feel I have served my purpose in this household. I can be of more use elsewhere."

Louisa opened her mouth again, but Abigail forestalled any further arguments. "If I keep dawdling, I will never finish my packing," she said, "and you girls must go dress for your dinner. I have never cared for this nonsense of being fashionably late, and believe that women of true elegance always try to be punctual."

Though it cost her dearly, Abigail managed to maintain her stern governess facade. She chased both girls out of her bedchamber. Only after Louisa and Clarice had gone, did she rest her forehead against the door, struggling against the burning sensation in her throat and eyes. She thumped her fist against the door panel.

If she did not take care, she was going to turn into one of these maudlin, sentimental creatures who wept upon every occasion. Drawing in a shuddering sigh, Abigail returned to her packing. Taking care no longer seemed of any importance. She scooped her belongings out of drawers, tossing everything haphazardly into the trunk.

Everything except for the green silk gown.

When she had done, Abigail slammed down the lid and went to peer out her bedchamber window. She had already sent word to her sister. Jane had promised to dispatch a carriage to fetch her. But the rain was coming down in such torrents, it was all but impossible to see into the street below.

Abigail could not recall such a rainstorm since that long-ago autumn afternoon in the folly at Ashdown. Nate had been so angry at her for spooking his horse, getting them both stranded and soaked.

Her lips curved into a smile of bittersweet remembrance, a smile that grew more tremulous as she recollected how Nate had first entreated her to be his friend.

"I have not yet found a friend in this country," he had said.

She had not either.

"And I doubt I ever will again, Mr. Harding," she murmured.

She had lived in fear she would regret that moment when she had permitted him to clasp her hand in friendship, but as it turned out, the regrets were not hers, but his.

This afternoon in the park, he had told her quite

plainly that he wished they had never met, that he would have been more content.

Despite the way her heart was aching, it was a wish she did not share. She was going to miss him, miss the stubborn way his jaw flexed when he defended his Yankee heritage, miss the devilish glint in his eyes when he was about to say something outrageous, miss the lightning flash of his smile that was so infectious . . . even miss discovering the sweet mystery of where his fire-hot kisses might have led.

But she had no choice except to go. She could not stay here, feeling that her presence made him unhappy, kept him apart from his family, even for the short interim that they would all remain in England.

He had tried to dissuade her from giving up her post, but not very hard, she thought. He had once told her that he would be damned before he'd allow the woman he loved to just walk away. Well, it was obvious Nate Harding did not love her. He'd made no effort to keep her from going to Windom's side today.

It only remained for Abigail to conquer her own feelings. She supposed that was not impossible. She'd survived such a thing once before. When parting from Windom, it had taken her, perhaps, six months to get over feeling completely desolate.

Given the strength of her attachment to Nate, it would likely take her only . . .

Only the rest of her life.

Abigail sighed and felt almost relieved when a light knock sounded on her door. She hoped it would prove to be word that her carriage had arrived. The sooner she wrenched herself free of the Harding household, the better.

Her heart sank when it was Lady Harding who slipped hesitantly across her threshold. It had been difficult enough earlier when Abigail had announced her intention of going to her ladyship. No rebukes, no awkward questions had escaped Helen's lips. She had merely regarded Abigail with an expression of deep sorrow.

Traces of that same sorrow remained as her ladyship glanced at Abigail's closed trunk. "Oh, you are already packed. I had hoped you might change your mind. At least you cannot be thinking of going this evening. Not in this pouring rain."

Abigail forced a smile to her lips. "I don't melt, my lady."

At least not in the rain. Only in Nate's arms.

Lady Harding gave a heavy sigh. "Well, you have a visitor, my dear. Lord Windom. I hinted that this was a most unseasonable hour, but he seems determined to see you. I cannot imagine what could be so urgent."

Abigail could. She had sensed in Windom's manner this afternoon, a man screwing up his courage to the sticking point. He must have finally come to propose. It had only taken him eleven years to make up his mind to do so. But Abigail feared she was little better when it came to decisiveness.

Once she'd been so certain of what she wanted, but now she scarce knew what she would say to his lordship. Windom represented a place to belong, a house of her own, security, things that she had once scorned her sister for seeking at any cost.

But matters took on a slightly different cast as one grew older. And Abigail still retained a certain *liking* for his lordship. But liking was a far cry from love, especially the kind of love she felt for Nate Harding.

Abigail fretted her lower lip, aware that Lady Harding still awaited her answer. What a pity the rain could not have kept Windom away a day longer. She might have felt more equal to dealing with his lordship then.

Her reluctance must have become obvious even to Lady Harding, for she said, "You don't have to see Lord Windom if you don't want to, my dear. I should be quite happy to tell him you are indisposed."

Abigail had a cowardly impulse to allow Lady Harding to do just that. But she would have to give Eliot an answer to his suit sooner or later.

"No, my lady," she said with an air of resignation. "Tell his lordship I will be down directly."

Nate stalked into the lower hall of the town house, rainwater dripping off his cloak onto the tiled floor. He stripped off the soaked garment and shook droplets off his curly-brimmed beaver before handing it off to the footman.

He noted that Nell had brought the ubiquitous Andrew with her from Ashdown Manor.

"How are you, sir?" the young footman beamed.

"Wet." Nate swiped cold beads of water from his chin. "Where is my stepmother?"

"Upstairs in the front drawing room, sir. Shall I—"

"No, I'll get the door. You take care of the hat." Pivoting on his heel, Nate charged toward the stairs, waving away the crusty butler who was worse than Andrew. The old man didn't think anyone should be allowed in Lady Harding's presence without being announced.

"Hellfire! Nell knows who I am," Nate snapped impatiently, starting to take the steps two at a time. He did not know what had induced Nell to send for him on such a foul evening, but Nate anticipated all manner of dire calamities.

His anxiety only sharpened when Louisa and Clarice met him halfway on the stairs, their faces flushed with distress.

"Oh, Nate, thank God you've come!" Louisa cried.

"What is it? What's wrong?" Nate asked. "Is something amiss with Nell?"

"No, it's Abby."

Abby. Nate's heart gave a sickened lurch. "What's wrong with Abby? What's happened to her? Is she ill?"

Without waiting for an answer, he thrust his sisters aside to charge the rest of the way upstairs.

"Nate, Abby is leaving us."

Clarice's sorrowful words stopped him cold in his tracks.

He felt his shoulders start to sag and stiffened them. "Yes, I already knew she wanted to do that."

"Did you also know that Lord Windom is here to see her?" Louisa asked.

"Windom?" Nate wondered if the sound of that man's name would always affect him like a jab with a red-hot poker.

"His lordship is with Abby now," Clarice said.

"In the back sitting room." Louisa added. "Lord Windom asked Mama if it was all right to speak to Abigail, and Mama let him."

Nate stifled an oath. Could his gentle stepmother ever say no to anyone? Nell should have chucked the priggish bastard out on his ear. There was no doubt in Nate's mind as to what Windom had come for, why he desired a private audience with Abigail.

The familiar fire of jealousy rushing through his veins, Nate bolted up two more steps only to stop again. No, Abigail would not be likely to thank him for bursting in upon her. Hadn't she been waiting for this moment for a long time? If Windom was the man she wanted, painful as the thought was, Nate had no right to interfere.

Coming about, he made his way despondently back down the stairs, past his staring sisters.

"Nate, where are you going?" Louisa asked.

"Back to my lodgings," he muttered, "to get quietly drunk."

He summoned Andrew to fetch his curly-brimmed beaver and cloak. But no sooner had the footman handed over Nate's hat, than Louisa was there, snatching it, swinging it out of Nate's reach.

"Don't you understand, Nate?" she demanded. "Lord Windom is upstairs with Abigail. *Alone.*"

"That's hardly any cause for alarm. Believe me, she's got nothing to fear from him," Nate said dryly.

"Yes, she does, you great dunderhead. Can you not figure out he must be proposing to her?"

"I am sure that is no concern of mine."

He saw Louisa and Clarice exchange a glance, and then Clarice spoke up, "Louisa and I are not entirely blind, Nate. We have some notion of what has been going on with you and Abigail. We are no longer children, you know."

Any other time her efforts to speak in such mature, sophisticated accents would have afforded

Nate a deal of tender amusement. But he had never felt less like laughing.

"We have been able to figure out why you really left Ashdown Manor so suddenly," Louisa added. "Of course, Mama forbade us to speak of it to you."

"Then don't." Nate reached for his hat again, but Louisa whipped it behind her back.

"Nate," Clarice said, "you cannot wish for Abby to marry Lord Windom. His lordship is—is a very noble gentleman, I am sure, but he is also . . ."

"He's also about as exciting as a soggy bisquit," Louisa finished.

"Abigail seems to prefer English biscuits to American hardtack." Dropping his manner of assumed indifference, Nate added quietly, "She loves Windom. She always has."

"No, she doesn't," Louisa said. "It's not his rose petals she saves."

Nate scowled at her. "What are you talking about, Lou?"

Louisa turned to give Clarice a nudge. "Tell him."

Clarice fixed Nate with earnest eyes. "When we were watching Abigail pack, she tried to hide something from us, but I saw what it was. Nate, she still has the flowers you gave her at Christmas, pressed between the pages of her books."

"And she was letting your rose petals fly all through her trunk, crumbling over her clothes," Louisa chimed in. "And you know how neat Abigail likes things. If that's not love, I'd like to know what is."

Nate gave his sister a baleful glare. In spite of himself, Louisa's idiotic notions stirred in him a fluttering of hope. He was quick to suppress it.

Shaking his head, he said, "Don't be ridiculous, Louisa. Windom is Abby's idea of perfection, not a roughneck Yankee who can't even contrive to control his temper."

"So you're just giving up?" Louisa asked.

"I don't see as I have any other choice."

"If Colonel Buckmeister and the minutemen had thought that way, I guess we'd all still be subjects of the king."

"Abby's a woman, not a parcel of land," Nate growled. "Now if you don't mind, I'd like my hat, Louisa. I've had about enough of being called out on this fool's errand."

Louisa stared back at him with a truculent scowl. But when he advanced upon her, she all but crammed the high-crowned beaver into his outstretched hands. "Here, then. Take your blasted hat. You are the fool, Nate Harding."

Though she said nothing, Clarice was looking no less disappointed in him. Ignoring them both, Nate strode toward the door. They were a pair of little idiots. Abigail would not want him fighting over her. She would only despise him for it.

But as his hand closed over the knob, somehow he could not seem to find the strength to turn it. He glanced toward the upper regions of the house, and his heart burned with the image of Abigail locked in Windom's stiff-necked embrace.

Don't do it, Abby, he wanted to beg her. It had taken Windom this many years to propose, and he was only doing it now when all was secure and proper and safe. What kind of passion was that?

Abigail had too much liveliness, humor, and intelligence, too much fire to waste herself on a man as spiritless as a Lord Eliot Windom. Maybe Nate didn't have the right to interfere as a lover, but he had been her friend once.

He still was.

Coming away from the door, he said, "Maybe I could just pop upstairs and speak to Abigail for a few moments."

Louisa and Clarice perked up at once. Louisa hastened forward to relieve Nate of his hat.

"I knew you would not just tamely slink away." She beamed. "Not my brother."

"And it will be so lovely to have Abby as a sister," Clarice said.

"Whoa! I can't promise anything like that. I will be fortunate enough to stop Abigail from marrying Windom."

"How are you going to do it?" Louisa asked.

Nate grimaced. "I haven't the damnedest notion."

"Well, I don't think you should actually fight with his lordship," Clarice said nervously.

"Yes, I suppose you had better at least try to be tactful, Nate," Louisa agreed.

"My dear Louisa, I spent four months campaigning to get you those cursed Almack tickets. I think I have learned a little something of the art of British diplomacy."

But as Nate turned to stride purposefully up the stairs, he was scarce aware himself that his hands were already tightening into a formidable pair of American fists.

Chapter 10

It had taken Eliot Windom eleven years to reach this moment, and the man still seemed unable to get to the point. Abigail sat upon a velvet-covered settee, her hands folded in her lap, trying not to fidget as Windom posed before her, his hands locked behind his back.

The sight of the candlelight playing over his perfectly chiseled features did nothing to ease her mood of despondency. He cleared his throat for perhaps the tenth time, and said, "That—that was a truly delightful time in the park this afternoon."

What was he talking about? Abigail wondered. The visit to the park had been wretched. All she recalled of it was her quarrel with Nate, and watching Nate stalk away from her.

When she regarded him questioningly, Windom reminded her, "The stroll you took with me and my daughters."

"Oh, that." She added hastily, "Yes, indeed, very pleasant. You have such charming little girls."

"Maria and Caroline were both quite enchanted with you."

"I always seem to get on well with children."

He cleared his throat. Again. "That brings me to the real purpose of my visit. I can wait no longer to unburden my heart to you."

Why not? He had already waited eleven years. But the thought struck Abigail with no rancor, no bitterness, rather only with some of Nate Harding's wry Yankee skepticism.

Windom paced off a few steps, taking in a deep breath. Abigail found herself almost wishing to stop him, but she remained silent as he dropped to one knee before her.

Taking one of her hands between his own, he favored her with his melancholy smile. "Look at me Abigail, as bashful as a schoolboy, and you can have no doubt as to why I am here."

She would have to be a little obtuse not to figure that out with him kneeling before her.

"I have adored you from the moment I first saw you. And my devotion has remained unchanged through all this time."

Even while you were married to your heiress? Nate's voice again, echoing in her head.

Abigail winced and tried to give Eliot her full concentration.

"Circumstances once kept us apart, kept me from declaring myself, but now I feel free to do so. Abigail, I beg you to become my wife."

"Are you sure there are still not some members of your family who would object to your wedding a governess?"

"A few of my sisters would snub me perhaps, but I should learn to bear it. My brother Clarence who is now the head of the family raised some slight objection, but I dared to inform him he had no right to forbid me."

"How bold of you."

She could not quite keep the sarcasm from her voice, and it was not lost on Windom. He chafed her hand lightly, looking a little downcast. "I am aware I must not seem to you the most ardent suitor, Abigail. But you of all people have ever understood my obligation to my family."

"Yes, I suppose I have."

"But I never forgot you. I have a confession to make. I did not turn up at Ashdown Manor by coincidence. I learned where you were employed and *contrived* to see you again."

"I am glad you at least waited until your wife was cold in her grave."

"Abigail!" Windom drew back looking shocked and hurt. "Of course, I observed a proper period of mourning for Catherine."

"I am sorry, Eliot. I am sure you did," Abigail said wearily. She rose from the settee and retreated toward the hearth. "I did not mean to sound ill-natured. It is just that—that I am feeling a little confused this evening."

"Confused. But—but I thought—that is I assumed that you felt as I do, that nothing has changed."

Could he not see it? Everything had changed. She was no longer the same impressionable young governess who had succumbed to the longing sighs of a handsome peer. She had often accused Nate of being opinionated, but it was shocking to realize how narrow her own views of the world had been.

"Does this mean you are refusing my suit?" Eliot asked wistfully.

"I—I don't know." Abigail pressed her hands to her forehead, feeling she was being incredibly foolish. She did believe that Eliot loved her, after his own fashion.

It just did not happen to be Nate Harding's fashion, the full-blooded, neck or nothing way that she knew Nate would love some fortunate woman someday.

But at least she did understand Eliot. He was a perfect gentleman. Even his little daughters were perfect. None of them would ever give her a single uneasy moment.

Unlike Nate, who had already given her plenty of them. And she cherished every one. Oh, she was indeed being idiotic. How did she know that Windom was not capable of stirring similar fires inside of her? She had never even been properly kissed by the man.

He came up behind her and rested his hand upon her shoulder. "Abigail, is there nothing that I can do or say that would help you to make up your mind?"

Giving way to an inexplicable impulse, she came about to face him. "Yes, one thing."

"Name it, my dear."

"Kiss me."

He looked astonished by the request. But when she tapped her foot impatiently, he bent to comply. Gently, he brushed his lips against hers. His kiss was very warm and sweet, but it was like expecting fireworks from a man who had no notion how to light the fuse.

Abigail gave a regretful sigh as their lips parted. She now knew exactly what she had to say to his lordship.

"You call that a kiss?"

The scornful male voice that echoed from the doorway startled both Abigail and Windom. They leaped apart, Abigail's gaze flying to where Nate loomed upon the threshold, his approach having gone quite undetected.

With his hair damp from the rain, his jaw jutting in that aggressive manner, his arms folded across his chest, he looked like some rugged windswept sailor bracing himself to defy a storm.

Joy at seeing him mingled in Abigail with mortification.

Windom had flushed beet red. "Sir! I am engaged in a most private interview with Miss Prentiss."

"So I see. Highly improper of you, my lord, Miss Prentiss. Being closeted together this way and no chaperon present."

Abigail nearly choked. "You—you dare to lecture Lord Windom on propriety after you . . . you—"

Nate quirked one brow as though challenging her to complete the thought, enlighten Windom as to what had occurred that night in her bedchamber.

"I have Lady Harding's permission to see Abigail alone," Lord Windom said.

"You don't have mine."

"I fail to see this is any of your concern, sir."

"We Yankees have a lamentable habit of not minding our own business." Nate strolled farther into the room, his lips tipped in a slight curve, an unholy light in his eyes. Despite her sense of outrage at his conduct, Abigail experienced a nervous flutter. Nate was never more dangerous than when he smiled that way.

He stalked toward her, saying softly, "So tell me,

Abby. What did you think of his lordship's kiss? I am perishing to know."

Abigail felt her cheeks flame. "Mr. Harding! How—how dare you!"

"Oh, pretty much the same way I dared before."

Before Abigail could draw breath, he seized her and bent her back over his arm. She had only time to voice a startled protest before Nate's mouth came down hard upon hers.

The man had run quite mad! He was kissing her right under Windom's very nose. Trying to break away, Abigail pummeled Nate's back with her fists. She was going to die of embarrassment. She was going to murder Nate Harding. She was going to—

A low moan escaped her as Nate's lips moved over hers, spreading fire through her veins, making her feel weak and dizzy. When he finally released her, she was gasping for breath and had to clutch the back of the settee for support.

Windom had stood by, too stunned to react. But now he stiffened with anger. "Sir, you—you have insulted Miss Prentiss."

His own breathing ragged, Nate regarded Abigail with a slow and seductive smile. "She doesn't look insulted to me."

Abigail could do no more than shoot him a reproachful glare.

"I shall send my second to wait upon yours, Mr. Harding," Windom said. "You will answer to me for this outrage."

"No, I won't. Pistols at dawn are not my style."

"Then you are refusing to give me satisfaction?"

"I didn't say that." Nate's teeth flashed in a feral grin.

Windom might look confused, but Abigail had no

difficulty in interpreting Nate's remark. She gave an alarmed cry as she saw him start to draw back his arm.

"Nate, no!"

She hurled herself in between the two men just as Nate's fist flashed out. The world seemed to explode about her in a fusion of light and pain as she felt rock-hard flesh and bone connect with her jaw.

She reeled for a moment, catching a glimpse of Nate's stricken expression.

"Abby!"

She staggered forward in his arms, the dancing lights fading into an all-encompassing darkness.

Nate paced Nell's drawing room like a caged timber wolf he'd once seen exhibited at a fair. It seemed like hours ago that he had scooped Abigail up in trembling arms and carried her to her bed. He'd just managed to allay his worst terrors. He hadn't killed her or broken her jaw. She had been beginning to come around when he had been driven off by Nell, his gentle stepmother for once amazingly stern.

"But I only want to—" he had tried to protest.

"I think you have done quite enough damage for one evening, Nathaniel."

Overcome with guilt, he'd been forced to agree. When Abigail did revive, he doubted that it was his face that she would want to see. He had hovered by her doorway long enough to receive the intelligence from Louisa that Abigail was able to sit up and take some tea.

Tea. The English cure-all for everything. Pity it could not cure a man of being an unutterable ass. Nate would swallow the stuff by the gallon.

He tugged at his cravat, destroying what remained of the starched linen folds. He had certainly done a bang-up job of it this time. Not only had he knocked Abigail unconscious, he had not even succeeded in routing Windom. The fellow was lurking in the house somewhere, probably sipping his own tea, having his ruffled feathers soothed by Nell.

As long as things had already ended in such disaster, Nate thought, he might as well have punched Windom out, too, just for the hell of it. For no other reason than the way the prig had embraced Abigail. A man who couldn't kiss a woman any better than that deserved to be walloped.

But Nate supposed that was the kind of thinking that gave Abigail such a disgust of him. And disgusted was too mild a word for what she must be feeling toward him now. He had gone the limits for boorish conduct this time, and she was not likely to ever forgive him. He sighed. He really had not meant for things to turn out this way. He had fully intended to be diplomatic, to reason Abigail out of marrying Windom.

But when he had heard her actually asking Windom for a kiss, his demon of jealousy had quite taken over. He'd hauled her into his arms determined that if she would persist in wanting to marry Lord Prim and Proper, at least Nate would show her what she would be missing.

And he'd shown her all right. Stretching his arm along the mantel, he felt like banging his head against the hard oak, but settled for resting his brow against it.

He remained oblivious when Abigail slipped quietly into the room a few moments later, closing the door behind her. Over Lady Harding's strenuous objections, Abigail had quit her bed, but she was no longer the least bit woozy.

In fact, Nate's blow had left her feeling remarkably clearheaded. She glanced across the room, taking in the details of Nate's haggard appearance, the dejected set to those strong, proud shoulders.

A smile escaped her, part tenderness and part exasperation. She winced almost immediately, gasping at the pain that throbbed along her jaw.

The sound, soft as it was, alerted Nate to her presence. He spun about, his face suffusing with both relief and guilt at the sight of her.

"Abby!" He started toward her. "Oh, God, I've darkened your daylights."

"Not quite, Mr. Harding. You only managed to level me."

He raised trembling fingers toward her cheek. Abigail's breath snagged in her throat. But he withdrew as though he feared one more touch from him would shatter her.

"I'm sorry, Abigail. I'd cut off my arm before hurting you. Hellfire, madam. You—you should have—"

"Stepped aside and let you engage in fisticuffs with Lord Windom? I do not think Lady Harding would wish a brawl conducted in her house, sir."

His blue eyes looked so haunted with remorse, it was all Abigail could do to maintain her disapproving facade. "Your behavior tonight was completely reprehensible."

"Yes, I know." He groaned. "I don't know what the devil got into me."

Abigail thought she had a fair idea, but she needed to hear him say it.

"All I ever wanted was for you to be happy, Abby. If I thought Windom could make you so, I would have just gone quietly away, I swear it." He dragged his hand back through his hair. "But something in me just can't tolerate the idea of you marrying that—that pattern card."

"Lord Windom is a most respectable, proper gentleman, sir."

"I think someday, Abigail, you will find that propriety makes for a very cold bed partner. I was only trying to save you from waking up someday and being very sorry."

"How noble of you."

"Not entirely. I had a few selfish motives, too."

"Oh?" Abigail's heart quickened as she waited.

Nate compressed his lips together then blurted out, "Damn it all, I love you and want to marry you myself."

A glad cry escaped Abigail, and she started to rush toward him. To her astonishment, Nate retreated.

"Of course, I know that's impossible, especially now," he said gruffly. "If you truly want to go to Windom, I won't try to stop you."

Abigail sighed. What was it going to take to penetrate Nate's thick wall of Yankee stubbornness?

"Mr. Harding, it so happens that I have no intention of marrying his lordship, not when I have fallen in love with you. I would marry you, but you have disappointed me. You once told me you would be damned before allowing the woman you loved to walk away."

She turned her back upon him. "It seems you are no better than an Englishman, after all."

Her heart hammering, Abigail started walking

toward the door. She had not taken two steps when she heard Nate's throaty growl.

His hands closed about her shoulders as he spun her about, yanking her into his arms. His face hovered above hers for a moment, his eyes glinting dangerously.

"No better than an Englishman, madam?" he hissed. "I'll show you."

His lips closed over hers so fierce and seeking, she stifled a gasp. Her aching jaw throbbed, but she didn't care. This time it did not even occur to Abigail to resist. She wound her arms about his neck, half laughing, half weeping as she returned his kiss.

Breathless moments later, he paused to glance down at her, his face dazed with joy and wonder. "You—you truly meant it? You do love me, Abby?"

"Yes, Nathaniel."

"And you would marry me?"

"Oh, yes, Nathaniel."

He buried his face in her hair with a blissful sigh. "You can't think how crazed I've been, thinking you were going to accept that idiot Windom."

"What about how miserable I have been? You said you were more content before you ever met me."

"So I was," Nate murmured wickedly. "But whoever wanted to be content? I could have ended up as placid and dull as your Eliot."

He stifled her indignant outcry with another kiss, only breaking the passionate contact when Abigail flinched. He brushed his lips lightly over the bruised area of her jaw.

"Abby," he said, "the next time I try to hit someone, promise you won't get in the way."

"The *next* time, sir!"

"Of course, there won't be a next time," he said hastily. "At least I will try to make certain there won't be."

The light shining in his eyes became earnest and solemn as he continued, "I mean to do my best to be the kind of man you can admire, Abigail. I'll settle here in England permanently, be the best damn lord that Ashdown Manor ever—"

She placed her hand over his lips to halt this flow of rash promises. If she had harbored any doubts about the extent of Nate's love for her, he had just dispelled them. She felt her eyes mist with unshed tears.

"I would never ask such a sacrifice of you, Nathaniel. I well know what being an American means to you. Of course, we will be going back to Philadelphia."

"No, Abby." He pressed a fervent kiss against her fingertips. "You are English. Your home—"

"I do not have a home. I have lived in many great and elegant houses, but I never truly belonged anywhere. Not until I was with you. Even if you wish to live in a tent in a desert, my home will be wherever you are."

He swallowed hard, his face glowing with such gratitude and love, Abigail's heart felt full to the point of aching.

"You would do such a thing for me, Abby? Follow me to America, knowing that the discord between our nations has only grown worse. I could be taking you to a land where there will be war."

"Never between us, and that is all that matters. At least none that we cannot settle in civilized fashion." She brushed a tender kiss against the stubborn cleft in his chin. "And I must confess, I have a great curiosity to see the land that bred a man such as you."

"What, obstinate, hardheaded, and opinionated?"

"No, strong, brave, generous, and true." She tangled her fingers through his ash gold strands. "You must only promise me one thing."

"And what is that, my love?"

"Never, ever to cut your hair again."

He stared at her with one of those expressions men get when they are totally baffled by the workings of the female mind. Abigail saw nothing for it but to kiss him again.

She was still locked in Nate's embrace when Louisa thrust her head into the room. The girl's face brightened immediately.

"Oh, famous!"

"Go away, baggage," Nate said with a mock growl.

But nothing would deter Louisa from bounding into the room and seizing first Abigail in an exuberant hug, then Nate, then Abby again.

"This is wonderful, Abby," she cried. "For you must be meaning to marry my brother, are you not? You would not have let him kiss you so otherwise. I told you he wasn't so bad when you got to know him."

Abigail regarded the girl almost diffidently. "It does not displease you then, the notion of having your former governess for a sister?"

"No, indeed. I cannot wait to tell Mama and Clarice. They will be so happy." Louisa prepared to dash back out, pausing at the threshold to add, "Besides this means I can return to America. I think Mama and Clarice want to stay at Ashdown

Manor, and Mama would never have let me go back with just Nate."

"Louisa!" Nate frowned at his sister. "You have spent the past nine months telling me how wonderful you find England."

"So I do. But after all, Nate," she added loftily before whisking out the door, "it isn't Pennsylvania."

Abigail could not help laughing at the dumbfounded expression on Nate's face, laughing so much that it hurt her jaw. But she completely forgot her pain, when Nate drew her back into his arms.

And for the next several moments, it did not matter where they were . . . Philadelphia, London. Nate and Abigail were quite lost in a world of their own.